72 Hours

La'Shayla Godfrey

www.theinkwellpublishingcompany.com

ISBN: 979-8-89502-010-4 (hardback) | 979-8-89502-009-8 (paperback) | 979-8-89502-008-1 (ebook)

Publication Data
Subjects: Apocalypse; Survival; Found Family
Keyword: What it means to stay human when the world falls apart
Short Description: A must-read for anyone who believes survival means more than staying alive—it means holding onto who you are.

This is a work of fiction inspired by the author's imagination and experiences. While elements of the story may draw from reality, any resemblance to actual persons, organizations, or events—beyond those intentionally referenced—is entirely coincidental.

Printed in the United States of America
1st Printing
Editor: Demetri D. Long
Cover Designer & Illustrator: La'Shayla Godfrey
Formator: Demetri D. Long

While 72 Hours explores themes of personal growth, self-discovery, and navigating life's transitions under extreme circumstances, neither the author nor The Inkwell Publishing Company condones the misuse or misinterpretation of this work to promote harm, intolerance, or divisive agendas. This story is meant to spark empathy, reflection, and thoughtful dialogue as readers engage with the characters' humanity and choices. We encourage readers to honor the complexity of each perspective represented. The Inkwell Publishing Company and the author disclaim any responsibility for actions taken by individuals or groups who distort the intentions of this narrative.

Chapter 1
The First Hour

Kasai always thought the end of the world would be louder. Explosions, screaming, sirens—like in the movies. But when it started, it was eerily quiet, as if the world was holding its breath.

She was sitting in her bedroom, scrolling through her phone, half-listening to the news on the TV in the background. Another report about people getting sick in the city. Some kind of flu, they said. She'd heard about it all week, but it felt distant, like something happening over there, not in her small town. Definitely not in her house.

Her mother's voice floated up the stairs. "Kasai, I'm heading to the hospital! Be back tonight!"

Kasai didn't look up from her phone. "Okay," she called back, not thinking much of it. Her mom was a nurse—this wasn't the first time she'd been called in for an emergency shift. But it was the last time Kasai would ever hear her voice.

The door slammed downstairs. Kasai stared at the front door for a long moment, feeling... something. She'd later wonder if that was the exact moment everything changed.

Thirty minutes later, the power went out.

At first, it was just annoying. Her phone battery was at 12%, and the Wi-Fi was down, which meant no streaming, no social media, and no way to distract herself from the creeping sense of unease growing in her chest. She grabbed a flashlight from her nightstand and wandered to the window.

The neighborhood looked normal at first glance. Houses lined up in perfect rows, driveways empty where people had left for work. But something felt off.

Then she saw it.

A figure was standing in the middle of the street. Motionless. Too still to be normal. Kasai squinted, trying to make out the details in the dim evening light. It was Mr. Reynolds, the old man who lived two houses down. He was wearing his usual flannel jacket and jeans, but his head was tilted at an unnatural angle like his neck couldn't quite hold the weight anymore.

"Mr. Reynolds?" Kasai whispered though she knew he couldn't hear her.

Suddenly, he moved.

Not just a step or a stumble—he lunged, disappearing from view like something had yanked him forward. Kasai's heart pounded in her chest. She pressed her face closer to the window, trying to see where he went. That's when she noticed the other figures.

More people. Standing still. Watching.

Her breath caught in her throat as one of them—the woman from across the street—snapped her head up, eyes wide and wrong. Milky white, like all the life, had been drained out of them.

Kasai stumbled back from the window, her mind racing. What the hell is going on?

Her phone buzzed in her pocket, nearly making her jump out of her skin. She yanked it out. It was a text from her mom.

MOM: Lock the doors. Don't let anyone in. I love you.

That was the last message Kasai ever got.

Her hands shook as she read it again and again. The power was out, but the TV downstairs had flickered back to life, powered by some emergency broadcast system. A loud, flat emergency tone echoed through the house, followed by a robotic voice.

"This is a national emergency. Please remain inside your homes. Lock all doors and windows. Do not approach infected individuals. Help will arrive in 72 hours. Stay alive."

Kasai's mouth went dry. Infected? This wasn't the flu. This wasn't anything close to normal.

A sudden crash from downstairs snapped her into action. Her heart hammered in her chest as she grabbed her flashlight and crept toward the staircase. The house felt too quiet, every creak of the floorboards under her feet amplified in the silence.

Another noise—glass shattering.

Someone was inside.

Kasai froze halfway down the stairs, her mind screaming at her to run, but her feet wouldn't move. She peeked through the banister and saw him—her neighbor, Mr. Reynolds. His flannel jacket was soaked in blood, his mouth hanging open in a twisted, slack-jawed grin. His eyes were those same milky white she'd seen from the window.

And he wasn't alone.

Two more figures stumbled in behind him, dragging their feet, leaving smears of blood on the hardwood floor. Kasai recognized one of them—Mrs. Patterson from next door. She'd given Kasai cookies last Christmas. Now her face was twisted in a grotesque snarl, her hands clawing at the air like she was searching for something to tear apart.

Kasai's breath came in shallow gasps. She had to get out. Now.

She backed up slowly, careful not to make a sound, but the old wooden stairs betrayed her. A loud creak echoed through the house.

Three heads snapped up in unison, their dead eyes locking onto her.

Kasai didn't think. She ran.

Back up the stairs, down the hall, into her bedroom. She slammed the door shut and shoved her desk against it, her heart racing so fast she thought it might explode out of her chest.

But the door wouldn't hold.

The first heavy thud rattled the frame, followed by another, louder this time. Kasai scanned the room, her eyes landing on the window. Second story. If she jumped, she'd probably break something. But if she stayed, she'd die.

Another crash. The door splintered.

Kasai didn't hesitate. She grabbed her backpack, stuffed it with whatever she could find—her flashlight, a water bottle, a pocketknife—and flung the window open. The cool night air hit her face as she climbed onto the ledge.

Behind her, the door finally gave way.

She didn't look back. She jumped.

The world tilted as she crashed onto the front lawn, pain shooting through her ankle as she rolled to a stop. She bit back a scream and scrambled to her feet, limping toward the street. Behind her, the creatures poured out of the broken front door, their eyes locked onto her like sharks sensing blood in the water.

Kasai ran.

Her body screamed in protest, but adrenaline pushed her forward. She sprinted down the street, dodging abandoned cars and stumbling over debris. The town she'd grown up in was unrecognizable—cars were crashed into telephone poles, houses were burning in the distance, and everywhere she looked, people were running.

Or worse, they weren't running at all.

The infected were everywhere, dragging people down, ripping into them with horrifying, wet sounds.

Kasai's mind was numb, her only thought was to move. She ducked into an alley, her breath ragged, her vision blurring. She couldn't stop. She had to find help.

But the emergency broadcast echoed in her mind.

"Help will arrive in 72 hours. Stay alive."

Seventy-two hours. Three days. That was all she had to survive.

Kasai clenched her jaw, wiping the sweat from her forehead. She didn't know what was happening, but she knew one thing for sure.

She wasn't going to die tonight.

Kasai's legs burned as she sprinted through the darkened streets, every shadow stretching long and menacing under the dim glow of flickering streetlights. Her heart thudded in her chest, each beat pounding louder than the sound of her ragged breathing. She forced herself to focus, to stay upright despite the sharp pain radiating from her ankle. Don't stop. Just keep moving.

The town felt alien like it had been swallowed by a nightmare and spat back out. She recognized the streets—the same ones she'd walked to school on, the same ones where her mom had taught her how to ride a bike. But now they were littered with overturned cars, broken glass, and blood.

So much blood.

Kasai ducked behind a parked SUV when she heard something—a low, guttural growl, followed by a wet, tearing sound. Peeking around the corner, she saw two of them hunched over a body in the middle of the street. She clamped a hand over her mouth to stifle a gasp. The creatures tore into the flesh with savage hunger, their jaws working mechanically like they didn't even realize what they were doing—or maybe they didn't care.

The body twitched.

Kasai's stomach lurched. She squeezed her eyes shut, willing the image away, but it was burned into her mind now. When she opened her eyes again, the creatures had stopped eating. They were sniffing the air.

Her blood ran cold.

Slowly, their heads turned toward her hiding spot.

Run.

Kasai bolted from behind the SUV, her shoes slapping against the pavement as she tore down the street. Behind her, she could hear them giving chase—the slap of bare feet, the inhuman screeches that echoed through the night. They were fast. Faster than they had any right to be.

She darted down a side street, her breath coming in short, panicked gasps. Her vision blurred at the edges, but she didn't dare slow down. She could feel them closing in, their presence like a physical weight pressing down on her.

She spotted an alleyway ahead—a narrow gap between two

brick buildings. Without thinking, she dove into it, her shoulder scraping painfully against the rough wall. She stumbled but managed to keep her footing, her fingers brushing against the cool metal of a door handle. She yanked it, but it was locked.

Think, Kasai, think!

Her eyes darted upward. A fire escape ladder hung just out of reach. She jumped, her fingers barely catching the bottom rung. She gritted her teeth and pulled herself up, muscles screaming in protest. As she scrambled onto the first platform, the creatures skidded into the alley below, their milky eyes locking onto her.

One of them leaped, its clawed hands swiping at her ankle. Kasai yanked her leg up just in time, the tips of its fingers grazing her sneaker. She didn't look back again. She climbed, faster than she thought possible until she reached the rooftop.

She collapsed onto the gravel, her chest heaving. The sounds of the creatures echoed up from the alley below, but they didn't try to climb. Not yet.

Kasai stared up at the night sky, her mind racing. What the hell is happening?

She pulled out her phone, her fingers trembling. The battery icon flashed red—5% left. She opened her messages, staring at the last text from her mom.

MOM: Lock the doors. Don't let anyone in. I love you.

Kasai bit her lip hard, trying to hold back the tears threatening to spill over. No. Not now. Focus.

She switched to her contacts, scrolling until she found her mom's number. She hit call, pressing the phone to her ear. It rang once. Twice.

Then it went to voicemail.

Kasai's throat tightened. She ended the call and tried again. And again. The same result each time.

Finally, she gave up, letting the phone fall into her lap. The screen dimmed, then went dark.

She was alone.

The emergency broadcast echoed in her mind, the robotic voice cold and unfeeling. "Help will arrive in 72 hours. Stay alive."

Three days.

Kasai wiped her eyes and forced herself to sit up. She couldn't stay here. The rooftop felt safe for now, but the creatures would figure it out eventually. And even if they didn't, she didn't have food or water.

She scanned the surrounding rooftops, looking for a path forward. The buildings were close together, their flat roofs connected by narrow gaps. She could jump across them if she was careful.

But where do I go?

Her mind flashed to the school on the other side of town. It had a sturdy metal fence around it, and maybe—just maybe—the cafeteria still had food. She wasn't sure if it was a good plan, but it was something.

Taking a deep breath, she stood up and adjusted her backpack. The weight of it felt reassuring, a small anchor in the middle of this chaos.

She took a few steps back, then sprinted toward the edge of the roof. Her heart leaped into her throat as she jumped, the empty space yawning beneath her. For a split second, she thought she wouldn't make it.

But then her feet hit solid ground. She stumbled but stayed upright.

One rooftop down.

Kasai kept moving, her body running on pure adrenaline. She jumped from building to building, her mind focused on one thing: survival.

But as she landed on the next roof, she froze.

She wasn't alone.

A group of people—three of them—stood at the far end of the rooftop. They looked as ragged and terrified as she felt, their clothes torn and bloodstained. One of them, a tall boy with messy brown hair, pointed a crowbar at her.

"Who the hell are you?" he barked.

Kasai raised her hands slowly. "I—I'm not infected," she stammered. "I'm just trying to survive."

The boy's eyes narrowed. The girl next to him, older with

sharp eyes and a makeshift bandage around her arm, whispered something in his ear.

Finally, he lowered the crowbar.

"Name's Kyle," he said gruffly. "You're lucky we didn't throw you off this roof."

Kasai swallowed hard. "I'm Kasai."

The older woman nodded. "Elara. And this here is Milo." She gestured to a younger boy, maybe sixteen, with grease-stained hands and a wary expression.

Kasai let out a shaky breath. For the first time since this nightmare began, she wasn't alone.

But as the sounds of the infected echoed in the distance, she realized something else.

The real danger wasn't just the monsters outside.

It was the people trying to survive.

And she wasn't sure who she could trust.

72 Hours

Kasai's heart pounded in her chest, louder now than the sounds of the infected in the distance. She kept her hands raised, glancing between the three strangers on the rooftop. The boy with the crowbar—Kyle—still eyed her like she was just another threat. His stance was rigid, his knuckles white as he gripped the metal tightly.

Elara, the older woman with the bandaged arm, was calmer, but her sharp gaze flickered over Kasai like she was dissecting her, searching for any sign of danger. The third one, Milo, stood slightly behind them, arms crossed, his eyes narrow with suspicion. He was younger than Kyle but didn't seem any less dangerous.

Kasai swallowed hard, trying to keep her voice steady. "I'm not infected," she said again, her breath visible in the cool night air. "I just... I'm just trying to find somewhere safe."

Kyle snorted, finally lowering the crowbar a fraction. "Safe? You think anywhere's safe now?" His voice was rough, edged with bitterness. "You're either dead or you're infected. That's all that's left."

"I'm neither," Kasai shot back, surprising herself with how

firm her voice sounded. "I'm alive. Just like you."

For a moment, no one spoke. The distant moans of the infected drifted up from the streets below, a grim reminder of the world they were all now trapped in.

Elara finally broke the silence, her voice softer but no less firm. "How'd you get up here?"

Kasai hesitated. She didn't know if she could trust them, but she also didn't have many options. "My house... it wasn't safe anymore. I ran. I climbed up the fire escape back there," she said, jerking her thumb over her shoulder toward the building she'd just crossed from. "I saw you guys, but I didn't mean to scare anyone. I just need somewhere to figure out what to do next."

Kyle exchanged a glance with Elara, his jaw tightening. Milo muttered something under his breath, but Kasai couldn't catch it.

Finally, Kyle stepped back, lowering the crowbar completely. "Fine," he grumbled. "But if you even look like you're turning, you're going off this roof."

Kasai let out a breath she hadn't realized she was holding. "Fair enough."

Elara gave her a small nod, then gestured toward a makeshift camp they'd set up near a rooftop door—a pile of blankets, a few water bottles, and what looked like a half-eaten can of beans. It wasn't much, but it was the closest thing to safety Kasai had seen all night.

She followed them cautiously, her body still tense, ready to run if she had to. They sat in a loose circle, the tension still thick in the air.

Milo finally spoke up, his voice low and sharp. "Where's your family?"

The question hit Kasai like a punch to the gut. She stared at her hands, picking at the dirt under her nails to avoid their eyes. "My mom... she was at the hospital when it started. I haven't heard from her since."

There was a brief silence, heavy with unspoken words. Elara's expression softened slightly, but Kyle just shook his head.

"Then she's gone," he said bluntly. "You need to accept that."

Kasai's jaw clenched. She wanted to argue, to scream that he was wrong, but the words caught in her throat. Instead, she just nodded stiffly, burying the surge of emotion deep down where it couldn't distract her.

"What about you?" she asked, turning the question back on them.

Kyle shrugged, his gaze distant. "Family's not important anymore."

Milo scoffed. "Didn't have much to lose anyway," he muttered, pulling his knees to his chest.

Elara didn't say anything, just stared out over the city, her eyes reflecting the distant fires that burned in the darkness.

For a while, they sat in silence, each of them lost in their own thoughts. The city below was a symphony of chaos—screams, sirens, and the inhuman shrieks of the infected echoing off the buildings.

Finally, Elara spoke, her voice breaking the heavy quiet. "We need a plan."

Kasai nodded, grateful for something to focus on. "I was thinking about heading to the school," she offered. "It's got fences, and maybe there's food in the cafeteria."

Kyle snorted. "The school's probably crawling with those things by now."

"Maybe," Kasai shot back, her temper flaring. "But sitting on this roof until we starve isn't exactly a great plan either."

Elara raised a hand, silencing them both. "We'll need supplies if we're going anywhere," she said, glancing at their meager stash. "Food, water, weapons."

Milo perked up at that, his eyes gleaming with something like excitement. "I know a place," he said. "There's an auto shop a few blocks from here. My uncle owns it. He's got tools, maybe even a generator. We could grab some stuff, maybe fix up one of the cars in the lot."

Kyle frowned. "And risk getting torn apart in the process?"

"We're not going to last long up here without supplies," Elara pointed out. "It's a risk either way."

Kasai nodded, feeling a flicker of hope. "If we're smart about it, we can make it."

Kyle looked like he wanted to argue, but finally, he sighed, running a hand through his messy hair. "Fine," he muttered. "But we move at dawn. It's too dangerous out there at night."

The group agreed, and the tension eased slightly as they settled down to rest. But Kasai knew sleep wouldn't come easily. She lay down on the cold rooftop, staring up at the stars, her mind racing with everything that had happened—and everything still to come.

The emergency broadcast echoed in her mind, its cold, robotic voice impossible to forget.

"Help will arrive in 72 hours. Stay alive."

Kasai clenched her jaw, determination hardening in her chest. She didn't know what the next three days would bring, but she knew one thing for sure.

She was going to survive.

The night passed in a blur of restless, broken sleep. Kasai woke several times to the sounds of distant screams or the guttural groans of the infected wandering below. Each time, her heart pounded in her chest, but she forced herself to stay quiet, listening intently until the danger passed.

When the first light of dawn crept over the horizon, painting the sky in shades of pink and orange, Kyle shook them awake.

"Time to move," he whispered, his voice rough from sleep.

Kasai sat up, her body stiff and aching from the hard rooftop. She rubbed her eyes and glanced around at the others. Elara was already packing their supplies, her movements efficient and calm. Milo stretched with a groan, his eyes still half-closed but alert.

They gathered their things quickly, double-checking their gear. Kasai adjusted her backpack, feeling the comforting weight of her flashlight and the small pocketknife she'd packed. It wasn't much, but it was better than nothing.

Kyle led the way to the rooftop door, his crowbar clenched tightly in his hand. He paused, pressing his ear against the metal surface, listening for any sounds on the other side.

When he was satisfied, he nodded and slowly pushed the door open.

The stairwell beyond was dimly lit by the weak morning light filtering through the broken windows. The air was thick with the metallic scent of blood and something fouler, something rotting.

They moved cautiously, their footsteps soft against the concrete steps. Every creak, every distant noise made Kasai's heart race, but she forced herself to stay calm, to focus on the task at hand.

When they reached the ground floor, Kyle held up a hand, signaling for them to stop. He peeked around the corner, then motioned for them to follow.

The streets were eerily quiet in the early morning light, the usual sounds of the city replaced by an oppressive silence. Kasai scanned the area, her eyes darting to every shadow, every flicker of movement.

They stuck to the alleyways, avoiding the main roads where the infected were more likely to roam. Kasai's pulse quickened with every step, but the adrenaline kept her moving, kept her focused.

As they neared the auto shop, Milo gestured toward a side entrance. "This way," he whispered. "The front's probably a mess."

They slipped inside, the door creaking softly as it swung shut behind them. The shop was dark, the air heavy with the scent of oil and rust.

Milo moved ahead, navigating the cluttered space with practiced ease. "Tools are in the back," he whispered, leading them through the narrow aisles.

Kasai followed closely, her eyes scanning the shadows for any sign of danger. Her heart pounded in her chest, but she kept her breathing steady, her grip tight on the handle of her flashlight.

When they reached the storage room, Milo pushed the door open and let out a low whistle. "Jackpot," he muttered.

The room was filled with tools, cans of fuel, and even a few unopened boxes of supplies. Kasai felt a flicker of hope. Maybe they had a chance after all.

They worked quickly, gathering everything they could carry. Kasai stuffed her backpack with bottled water, a small first aid kit, and a heavy wrench that felt solid in her hands.

Just as they were finishing, a loud crash echoed from the front of the shop.

Kasai's blood ran cold.

Kyle cursed under his breath, tightening his grip on the crowbar. "They're here," he whispered.

The infected had found them.

Kasai's heart pounded in her chest as they huddled in the storage room, the sounds of shuffling footsteps and guttural growls growing louder.

They were out of time.

And the real fight was just beginning.

Kasai's heart raced as the sounds of the infected echoed through the auto shop—scraping feet, low, guttural growls that vibrated in her chest. The flickering light from a broken ceiling fixture cast eerie shadows across the room, turning the tools hanging on the walls into sharp, menacing shapes. She clutched the heavy wrench tighter, the cold metal grounding her in the rising panic.

Kyle was already moving, his crowbar gripped like an extension of his arm. "We need to find another way out," he hissed, his voice low but urgent. His eyes darted to Milo. "You said there's a back exit, right?"

Milo nodded, his face pale but determined. "Yeah. Through the garage, but..." His voice trailed off, and he swallowed hard. "If they're in the front, they're probably everywhere."

Elara moved closer, her face calm despite the fear in her eyes. "Then we don't have a choice. We move fast, stay quiet, and don't engage unless we have to."

Kasai nodded, even though every muscle in her body screamed to run, to bolt out the nearest door, and never look back. But she knew that was suicide. She had to stay with the group. Alone, she wouldn't last an hour.

Kyle cracked the door open just a fraction, peering through the gap. His jaw tightened. "Two of them, near the front counter. They haven't seen us yet."

Kasai's breath caught in her throat. She could almost picture them—the blank, milky eyes, the blood-smeared mouths. She forced herself to stay focused, to push the fear down.

Kyle closed the door softly and turned back to them. "We'll head for the garage. Milo, you're with me. Elara, Kasai—you two cover our backs."

Kasai nodded, her fingers tightening around the wrench. She didn't trust Kyle—not fully—but right now, he seemed to know what he was doing. And that was good enough.

They moved out in a tight line, their footsteps barely making a sound on the oil-slick floor. The shadows seemed to press in around them, the silence between the growls almost worse than the noise itself. Every creak, every distant scrape of metal, sent a jolt of adrenaline through Kasai's veins.

As they neared the garage, the faint smell of gasoline filled the air, mingling with the metallic tang of blood. Milo reached for the door, his hand trembling slightly as he gripped the handle.

And then—

A loud crash echoed from the front of the shop.

Kasai's heart leaped into her throat. The infected had heard something. They were moving, fast. The sounds of shuffling footsteps turned into pounding, urgent slaps against the concrete floor.

Kyle cursed under his breath. "Move! Now!"

Milo wrenched the garage door open, and they spilled into the large, open space beyond. The morning light poured in through cracked windows, illuminating the rows of cars and scattered tools. But Kasai barely had time to take it in before the first infected burst through the door behind them.

It was a man—at least, it had been. His clothes hung in tatters, blood smeared across his face and chest. His jaw hung at an unnatural angle, and his eyes... those empty, soulless eyes locked onto Kasai.

She didn't think. She swung the wrench with all her strength.

The metal connected with a sickening crack, and the creature collapsed in a heap at her feet. But there were more. Dozens of them, poured into the garage like a flood.

"Go!" Kyle shouted, swinging his crowbar in wide, brutal arcs. "Get to the exit!"

They ran. Kasai's lungs burned, her legs screaming in protest, but she didn't stop. She couldn't. She darted between cars, the sounds of the infected growing louder behind her.

Milo reached the back door first, slamming his shoulder into it. It didn't budge.

"It's stuck!" he shouted, panic rising in his voice.

Kyle was there in an instant, ramming his crowbar into the doorframe and prying with all his strength. The wood groaned, then splintered, and the door flew open.

Kasai and Elara barreled through, the sunlight blinding after the dimness of the garage. They stumbled into the alley behind the shop, the cool morning air burning in their lungs.

But they weren't safe yet.

The infected were right behind them, their shrieks echoing off the brick walls.

Kyle slammed the door shut, jamming the crowbar through the handle to buy them a few precious seconds. "Move! Don't stop!"

They sprinted down the alley, their footsteps pounding against the pavement. Kasai's vision blurred with sweat and exhaustion, but she kept going, fueled by sheer terror.

They burst out onto a side street, the city sprawled out before them in chaos. Fires burned in the distance, thick black smoke rising into the sky. Abandoned cars littered the streets, some still smoldering from crashes. The world Kasai had known was gone, replaced by this hellscape.

Kyle didn't slow down. He led them across the street, weaving between wreckage and debris until they reached an old apartment building. He kicked the door open, ushering them inside.

Kasai collapsed against the wall, gasping for breath. Her heart hammered in her chest, but they were safe—for now.

Elara was already checking the door, making sure it was secure. Kyle leaned against the wall, his chest heaving, while Milo paced nervously, his eyes darting to the windows.

Kasai let her head fall back against the cool brick. She closed her eyes, just for a moment, trying to process everything that had happened.

But the emergency broadcast echoed in her mind, a chilling

reminder of the nightmare they were trapped in.

"Help will arrive in 72 hours. Stay alive."

Kasai opened her eyes, her jaw set with grim determination.

They had supplies now, but this was only the beginning. The real challenge was surviving the next three days—and figuring out who they could trust.

Because the infected weren't the only threat out there.

And Kasai wasn't going to let anyone—or anything—take her down.

Kasai's breathing slowed as the adrenaline began to ebb, leaving her limbs heavy and her mind spinning. She stared at the peeling wallpaper of the apartment's narrow hallway, trying to process everything that had just happened. The world outside was a war zone, but here, for this fleeting moment, it was quiet.

Kyle paced near the door, peeking through the slats of the blinds, his crowbar still clutched tight in his hand. His knuckles were white, but his face was calm—or at least as calm as anyone could be in the middle of an apocalypse.

Elara was already moving through the room with a kind of quiet efficiency, checking for exits, locking windows, andsecuring anything that could be a weak point. Kasai admired her calmness. It wasn't the calm of someone who didn't care—it was the calm of someone who had seen too much to be surprised anymore.

Milo hovered near the kitchen, rifling through drawers and cabinets, his expression tight with frustration. "Nothing here," he muttered, slamming a cupboard shut. "Place has been picked clean."

Kasai finally peeled herself off the wall, her muscles protesting as she stood. She tightened her grip on the wrench, feeling the weight of it in her hand. It was comforting in a strange way—something solid, something she could rely on when everything else was falling apart.

"We can't stay here long," Kyle muttered, still watching the street below. "They'll be out there, and they'll find us eventually."

Elara nodded, her eyes scanning the apartment. "We need somewhere more secure. Somewhere we can hold up until... until we figure out what's really going on."

The words hung in the air, heavy and unspoken. No one wanted to say what they were all thinking: What if help isn't coming?

Kasai's mind flashed back to the broadcast, the robotic voice echoing in her head. "Help will arrive in 72 hours. Stay alive."

Seventy-two hours. It felt like an eternity.

Milo kicked at an empty can on the floor, his frustration boiling over. "This is insane. Are we just supposed to sit around and wait? For what? The army? The government? They're probably dead like everyone else."

Kyle's jaw tightened, but he didn't argue. Kasai could see it in his eyes—he was thinking the same thing.

"We need a plan," Elara said firmly, cutting through the tension. "We can't just wander around hoping we don't get eaten."

Kasai took a deep breath, forcing herself to focus. "I still think the school's our best bet. It's fenced in, and there's a kitchen. Maybe even first aid supplies."

Kyle snorted, shaking his head. "You don't know that. And it's probably crawling with those things by now."

"Maybe," Kasai shot back, her frustration flaring. "But staying here is just as dangerous. We need food, water, and a place we can actually defend."

Elara nodded thoughtfully. "She's right. The school's worth checking out. But we need to be smart about it."

Kyle sighed, rubbing a hand through his messy hair. "Fine. But we're not rushing in blind. We'll scout it out first. If it looks bad, we find somewhere else."

Kasai nodded, relief washing over her. At least they had a plan now. It wasn't much, but it was something to hold onto.

They spent the next hour gathering what little supplies they could find. Milo managed to scrounge up a half-empty box of granola bars and a dusty bottle of water from a forgotten pantry shelf. Elara found a first aid kit with a few bandages and a small bottle of antiseptic. It wasn't much, but it was better than nothing.

Kasai repacked her bag, making sure everything was secure.

The weight of the supplies on her back felt both reassuring and ominous. Every item was a reminder of the world they'd lost—and the fight ahead.

By the time they were ready to move, the sun was high in the sky, casting harsh shadows across the ruined city. The sounds of the infected had faded for now, but Kasai knew they were still out there, lurking just beyond sight.

Kyle led the way, his crowbar gripped tightly in his hand. They moved quickly and quietly, sticking to the alleyways and side streets, avoiding the main roads where the infected were more likely to roam.

Kasai's heart pounded with every step, her eyes scanning the shadows for any sign of movement. The city felt like a ghost town—silent, empty, but full of unseen dangers.

As they neared the school, they paused at the edge of a parking lot, crouching behind an overturned car. The building loomed ahead, its tall chain-link fence still intact, the front doors hanging slightly ajar.

Kyle pulled out a pair of binoculars he'd scavenged from the apartment, scanning the area. "I don't see any of them," he murmured, his voice low. "But that doesn't mean they're not inside."

Kasai's pulse quickened. The school looked quiet—too quiet. But it was their best shot.

Elara glanced at Kyle, then at Kasai. "We move fast. In and out. If it's clear, we set up camp. If not, we fall back."

They nodded in agreement, the plan set.

Milo found a gap in the fence where the metal had been bent back, just wide enough for them to slip through one at a time. Kasai went last, her heart pounding as she slid through the narrow opening, the cool metal scraping against her arm.

They approached the school cautiously, their footsteps barely making a sound on the cracked pavement. The front doors creaked as Kyle pushed them open, the sound echoing through the empty halls.

Inside, the school was eerily silent. The fluorescent lights flickered overhead, casting a sickly glow on the linoleum floors.

Lockers stood open, their contents spilled across the ground.

They moved through the halls in a tight formation, checking classrooms and storage rooms as they went. The tension was suffocating, every creak and groan of the old building setting Kasai's nerves on edge.

But so far, nothing. No infected. No signs of recent activity.

It was almost too good to be true.

They finally reached the cafeteria, and Kasai felt a surge of hope as they pushed open the double doors. The room was empty, but the shelves in the kitchen looked promising.

Milo whooped quietly, grinning as he rifled through the cabinets. "Jackpot!" he whispered, holding up a box of canned goods.

For the first time in what felt like forever, Kasai allowed herself to hope. Maybe they could survive this. Maybe they'd found a safe place, even if just for a little while.

But then—

A loud crash echoed from somewhere deep within the school.

Kasai's heart froze. The sound of shuffling footsteps followed, growing louder, *closer.*

They weren't alone.

Kyle cursed under his breath, tightening his grip on the crowbar. "Get ready," he whispered.

Kasai raised her wrench, her hands trembling. The infected were here, and they were coming fast.

The fight wasn't over.

Chapter 2
First Blood

The sound echoed through the cafeteria like a gunshot, a sharp metallic crash followed by the unmistakable shuffling of footsteps—too many footsteps.

Kasai's heart leaped into her throat as she clutched the wrench tighter in her sweaty palms. The quiet sense of relief that had been building since they'd found the untouched food evaporated in an instant. The infected were here. Now.

Kyle swore under his breath, his eyes darting toward the doors. "We need to move. Now."

"But the food—" Milo protested, his hands still half-buried in a box of canned beans.

"Screw the food!" Kyle snapped, his voice low but sharp enough to cut through the rising panic. "We'll come back for it if we can. But we won't be eating anything if we're dead!"

Kasai's pulse roared in her ears as she followed Kyle's lead, edging toward the side exit of the cafeteria. Her eyes flicked to Elara, who gave her a small, grim nod as she shouldered her backpack. Milo hesitated, his gaze torn between the precious supplies and the impending danger, but one more crash—closer this time—was enough to snap him into action.

They slipped out of the cafeteria, and back into the darkened hallways of the school. The fluorescent lights flickered overhead, casting long, jittery shadows on the walls. The air was thick with the smell of dust, old sweat, and something worse—the coppery tang of blood that clung to the back of Kasai's throat.

Kyle led them down the hall, moving with the kind of focused intensity that screamed experience. Kasai didn't know what his life had been before the world went to hell, but she could tell he'd seen things—done things. And right now, that made him the best person to follow.

But even Kyle's confidence couldn't change the fact that they were trapped.

The sounds of the infected grew louder with every step they took—shuffling feet, wet gasps, and the occasional guttural snarl that made Kasai's skin crawl. It wasn't just one or two of them. It was a horde.

"Stairs," Elara hissed, pointing toward a door at the end of the hallway. The small rectangular window set into the door showed a dim stairwell beyond, the kind that led to either salvation or a dead end.

Kyle didn't hesitate. He yanked the door open, and they piled inside, the heavy door slamming shut behind them with a thud that felt too loud in the oppressive silence that followed.

They paused for a breath, the narrow stairwell wrapping around them like a coffin. The echoes of the infected in the hall were muffled now, but Kasai knew it was only a matter of time before they figured out where the noise had gone.

"Up or down?" Milo whispered, his voice barely audible over the sound of their labored breathing.

Kyle's jaw clenched. "Up. Roof access."

Kasai swallowed hard. The idea of being trapped on another rooftop didn't exactly thrill her, but it was better than being cornered in a basement with no way out. She nodded, and they started climbing.

The stairwell was dark, the emergency lights flickering just enough to make the shadows seem alive. Every creak of the old metal steps made Kasai's heart pound harder. She tried to focus on her breathing, on keeping her steps light, but the weight of the wrench in her hand felt heavier with every flight they climbed.

They were halfway to the top when they heard it.

A door slammed open below them.

Then the sound of feet—running feet—pounding up the stairs after them.

Kasai's blood ran cold. These weren't the slow, shuffling infected they'd seen outside. These things were fast.

"Move!" Kyle barked, his voice tight with urgency.

They sprinted up the stairs, their footsteps echoing wildly in the narrow space. Kasai's lungs burned, but she pushed herself harder, the fear of what was behind them stronger than the pain in her chest.

They reached the top landing just as the infected rounded the corner below, their faces twisted in grotesque masks of hunger and rage.

Kyle slammed his shoulder into the door to the roof. It didn't budge.

"Locked!" he spat, stepping back to ram it again.

Kasai didn't think. She surged forward, her wrench raised high and brought it down with all her strength on the old metal handle. The brittle metal snapped under the force, and the door flew open with a screech of rusty hinges.

They spilled out onto the rooftop, the harsh afternoon sun blinding after the dimness of the stairwell. The hot asphalt burned through the soles of Kasai's shoes as they stumbled forward, slamming the door shut behind them.

Kyle jammed a metal rod through the door handles, buying them a few precious seconds. But it wouldn't hold for long.

Kasai turned in a slow circle, her chest heaving as she took in their surroundings. The rooftop was flat and barren, surrounded by a low chain-link fence. There were no fire escapes, and no adjacent rooftops close enough to jump to.

They were trapped.

"Over there!" Milo shouted, pointing toward a maintenance shed on the far side of the roof.

It wasn't much, but it was better than nothing. They sprinted across the rooftop, the sound of the infected pounding on the stairwell door behind them like a war drum.

They dove into the shed, slamming the flimsy door shut and barricading it with whatever they could find—an old mop handle, a rusted toolbox, anything to slow the inevitable.

Kasai collapsed against the wall, her chest burning as she tried to catch her breath. The walls of the shed felt too close, the air hot and stifling.

"We're trapped," Milo whispered, his voice trembling. "We're gonna die up here."

"No," Kasai snapped, more forcefully than she felt. "We're not. We just need to think."

Kyle paced the small space, his face a mask of frustration. "There's nothing to think about. We're stuck."

Elara, who had been silent until now, finally spoke. "We're not dead yet." Her voice was calm, and steady, like she was reminding them of something they'd forgotten. "We've survived this long. We can survive a little longer."

Kasai latched onto that thought, forcing herself to believe it. She wasn't ready to die. Not here. Not like this.

The pounding on the stairwell door grew louder, more frantic. The metal groaned under the pressure, and Kasai knew it was only a matter of time before it gave way.

But they weren't going down without a fight.

She tightened her grip on the wrench, her jaw set with grim determination.

Whatever came through that door, she was ready.

The pounding grew louder, a relentless, rhythmic assault that made Kasai's skin crawl. Each slam against the stairwell door reverberated through the rooftop, echoing off the walls of the maintenance shed like a heartbeat speeding toward panic. The infected weren't giving up. They never gave up.

Kasai tried to steady her breathing, pressing her back against the cold metal wall of the shed. The wrench in her hand felt heavier with each passing second, as though it absorbed her fear. She glanced around the small, claustrophobic space. Milo was crouched near the door, his eyes darting from the flimsy barricade to Kyle, who paced like a caged animal. Elara sat with her back to the opposite wall, her face pale but calm, her hands wrapped tightly around the handle of a rusted screwdriver.

They were out of time.

A loud crack split the air as the stairwell door finally gave way. The sound of the infected spilling onto the rooftop was unmistakable—the scrape of dragging feet, the guttural growls, and the horrifying slap of bare flesh against hot asphalt.

"They're here," Milo whispered, his voice trembling.

Kyle stopped pacing, his face hardening. "We hold them off as long as we can," he said, his voice low but steady. "If they get in, we don't let them take us easily."

Kasai's heart hammered in her chest, but she nodded. She wasn't ready to die—not yet. Not like this.

For a moment, there was silence, a tense, suffocating quiet as they waited. Then the infected found them.

The shed door shuddered under the first impact, the wood creaking as something heavy slammed against it. Kasai bit down a scream as splinters flew from the frame. The makeshift barricade of cleaning supplies and old tools rattled under the force, but it held—barely.

"They'll break through in seconds," Elara hissed, her eyes scanning the small space for anything else they could use.

Milo scrambled toward the back wall, his hands feeling around the edges. "Wait... wait!" he hissed. "There's a hatch here!"

Kasai spun around, her eyes widening as Milo tugged at a small, rusted trapdoor near the floor. It looked like it hadn't been used in years, but it was something.

"Help me!" he grunted, pulling with all his strength.

Kasai dropped her wrench and grabbed the edge of the hatch, her fingers slipping against the rust. Kyle was there a second later, and together, they yanked it open with a loud screech of protesting metal. A narrow, rusted ladder led down into darkness.

"It's a maintenance shaft," Milo panted, peering into the hole. "Might lead to the lower floors—or at least somewhere safer than here."

They didn't have time to debate. The shed door buckled under another hit, the wood splitting down the middle.

"Go!" Kyle barked.

Milo slid down the ladder first, disappearing into the shadows below. Kasai followed, her heart pounding as she climbed down into the dark. The air was thick with dust and the sharp scent of rusted metal, but it was cooler here, the sounds of the rooftop chaos muffled above her.

Elara came next, her face tight with concentration as she navigated the narrow ladder. Kyle was last, slamming the hatch shut above them just as the shed door gave way with a final, splintering crash.

They held their breath in the dark, listening to the muffled sounds of the infected swarming the shed above. For a moment, it felt like they'd made it. But the relief was short-lived.

The maintenance shaft was cramped and suffocating, the metal walls slick with condensation. Kasai's flashlight flickered weakly as she adjusted her grip on it, casting long, jittery shadows down the tunnel.

"Which way?" Kyle whispered, his voice barely more than a breath.

Milo pointed to the left, where the tunnel sloped downward. "That way. It should lead to the boiler room or the lower maintenance levels."

Without another word, they moved. The shaft was narrow, forcing them to crawl on their hands and knees. Every scrape of metal against metal echoed louder than it should have, and Kasai's heart pounded with every inch they moved forward.

The tunnel stretched on endlessly, the air growing colder and heavier the deeper they went. Kasai's knees ached from the rough metal floor, but she didn't dare slow down. She could still hear the faint, distant sounds of the infected above—like shadows chasing them through the dark.

Finally, after what felt like hours, the tunnel opened into a larger space. They tumbled out of the shaft and into an old boiler room, the air thick with the scent of rust and mildew.

Kasai scrambled to her feet, her flashlight sweeping over the room. It was large, filled with rusting machinery and tangled pipes. The walls were lined with old tools and dusty maintenance logs, and a heavy metal door stood on the far side, slightly ajar.

Kyle slammed the shaft door shut, wedging a rusted pipe through the handle to keep it sealed. For the first time since they'd entered the school, there was silence.

Kasai leaned against the cold wall, her chest heaving as she tried to catch her breath. Milo sank to the floor, his hands trembling as he wiped sweat from his brow.

"We made it," Elara whispered, her voice a mix of exhaustion and disbelief. "We actually made it."

But Kyle didn't look relieved. He was staring at the heavy metal door on the far side of the room, his jaw clenched.

Kasai followed his gaze, her stomach twisting. "What is it?"

Kyle didn't answer right away. He moved toward the door, his crowbar raised, and nudged it open with the tip.

The hallway beyond was dark, but the faintest hint of light flickered at the far end—and something else.

A low, rasping sound echoed down the corridor, followed by the soft, wet slap of footsteps.

Kasai's blood ran cold. They weren't alone down here.

Kyle stepped back, his face pale but determined. "We can't stay here. We have to keep moving."

Kasai's heart pounded, but she nodded. There was no choice. The infected were everywhere—above them, behind them, and now... below them.

They gathered their things quickly, their movements quiet and deliberate. Kasai adjusted the strap of her backpack, her fingers brushing against the cool metal of her wrench. It felt like the only thing keeping her grounded.

As they slipped into the dark hallway, Kasai felt a surge of grim determination. The world had gone to hell, but she wasn't going to die here—not in some forgotten basement, not without a fight.

The emergency broadcast echoed in her mind once more, a chilling reminder of the ticking clock hanging over their heads.

"Help will arrive in 72 hours. Stay alive."

Kasai clenched her jaw, pushing forward into the dark. The infected were coming. The world was falling apart.

But she was still here.

And she wasn't giving up.

The hallway stretched ahead like the throat of some enormous beast, dark and damp, with flickering emergency lights casting shadows that danced and shifted along the cracked concrete walls. Every step Kasai took echoed, despite her efforts to move silently. The others followed close behind—Kyle with his crowbar gripped tightly, Elara moving with quiet, measured precision, and Milo bringing up the rear, his breathing fast and uneven.

The low rasping sounds grew louder, more distinct. It wasn't just one infected. Kasai could hear the irregular rhythm of multiple footsteps, the wet slap of bare feet dragging across the floor mixed with the occasional guttural growl.

"We can't keep walking blind," Kyle whispered, his voice tense. "We need to know how many are up ahead."

Kasai nodded, swallowing the lump in her throat. She raised her flashlight, careful to shield most of its beam with her hand to avoid drawing too much attention. The narrow cone of light flickered as it pushed back the darkness.

Her breath caught in her throat.

There were at least four of them. Their bodies were hunched, limbs twisted in unnatural angles as they shambled toward the faint light at the far end of the corridor. Their skin was pale, almost translucent, stretched taut over bones and muscles that moved in jerky, erratic motions. But what froze Kasai in place was their eyes—cloudy and dead, yet somehow still aware.

One of the creatures stopped, its head snapping toward them with an unnatural speed. Its nostrils flared, and it let out a wet, guttural snarl.

"They know we're here," Kasai whispered, her voice barely audible over the sound of her pounding heart.

Before anyone could react, the creature let out a piercing scream, a sound so raw and primal it sent chills down Kasai's spine. The others responded instantly, their slow shamble turning into a sprint.

"Run!" Kyle shouted.

They bolted down the corridor, their footsteps pounding against the concrete floor. The infected were fast—too fast—and their snarls echoed off the walls, mixing with the frantic sounds of Kasai's own breathing.

They rounded a corner and nearly collided with a rusted metal door, its surface covered in peeling paint and deep scratches that looked disturbingly like claw marks. Kyle didn't hesitate. He slammed his shoulder into the door, forcing it open with a loud screech of metal on metal.

"Inside!" he barked, ushering them through.

Kasai dove into the room, her heart racing as she stumbled over debris scattered across the floor. Milo and Elara followed close behind, and Kyle slammed the door shut, jamming his crowbar through the handle to barricade it.

For a moment, there was only the sound of their ragged breathing. Then the infected hit the door.

The force of the impact rattled the entire frame, and Kasai could see the metal starting to bend under the pressure. The creatures on the other side snarled and screamed, their clawed hands scraping against the door with a sound that made her teeth ache.

"This won't hold for long," Kyle panted, his eyes darting around the room.

Kasai's flashlight flickered as she swept it across their surroundings. It looked like an old maintenance office—desks overturned, filing cabinets rusted and broken, papers scattered everywhere. But what caught her attention was the large air vent near the ceiling, its metal grate hanging loose.

"There!" she gasped, pointing toward the vent. "We can crawl through!"

Kyle's eyes followed her beam, and he nodded sharply. "Milo, help me get that open!"

While the two of them worked to pry the grate loose, Kasai moved to help Elara, who was rifling through one of the cabinets. Her hands were shaking, but her movements were purposeful as she pulled out a small toolkit and shoved it into her bag.

"Never know when this might come in handy," Elara muttered, forcing a tight smile that didn't reach her eyes.

Kasai nodded, her throat too dry to respond. She could hear the infected battering against the door, the metal groaning louder with each hit. They were running out of time.

"Got it!" Milo shouted.

Kyle ripped the vent cover free and tossed it aside. "Kasai, you go first. Elara, you're next. Milo, you're after her. I'll bring up the rear."

Kasai didn't argue. She scrambled onto the desk beneath the vent, hoisting herself up with shaking arms. The metal was cold against her skin as she pulled herself into the narrow tunnel, the sharp edges biting into her palms. She pushed forward, the darkness pressing in from all sides.

The air in the vent was thick with dust and the metallic scent of rust. It was a tight fit, and Kasai's shoulders scraped against the sides as she crawled. She could hear the others following close behind, their breathing loud in the confined space.

Then the door below gave way.

The sound of it crashing open echoed through the vent, followed by the snarls of the infected as they poured into the room. Kasai's heart pounded in her ears as she crawled faster, her elbows and knees screaming in protest.

She could hear Kyle grunting below, the sound of his crowbar meeting flesh and bone. The infected shrieked in rage, and Kasai's breath caught in her throat.

"Kyle!" Milo shouted.

"Keep moving!" Kyle roared back. "Don't stop!"

Kasai forced herself forward, tears stinging her eyes as she crawled faster, the metal scraping against her skin. She couldn't stop. She wouldn't stop.

The vent sloped downward, and Kasai felt her body slide forward, gaining speed. She saw a faint light ahead—a grate leading into another room. She braced herself and kicked, the metal giving way with a loud clang as she tumbled out onto the floor below.

Elara and Milo followed seconds later, landing in a heap beside her. They scrambled to their feet, turning to help Kyle.

But Kyle didn't come.

Kasai stared at the vent, her heart pounding in her chest. "Kyle?" she whispered, her voice trembling.

For a moment, there was only silence. Then they heard it—a final, guttural scream, cut off by a sickening crunch.

Milo let out a strangled sob, his hands clenched into fists. Elara's face was pale, her eyes wide with shock.

Kasai felt like the air had been knocked out of her lungs. She wanted to scream, to cry, but there was no time. The infected would be on them soon.

"We have to move," Elara whispered, her voice hollow.

Kasai nodded numbly, forcing herself to stand. She grabbed her wrench, the cold metal grounding her as she turned away from the vent.

They had lost Kyle. But they were still alive.

And they had to keep going.

Because the clock was still ticking.

And they had 71 hours left to survive.

The weight of Kyle's absence pressed down on Kasai like a boulder, heavy and suffocating. The echo of his last scream still rang in her ears, a raw reminder of how quickly everything could spiral into chaos. But there was no time to grieve. The infected were relentless, and they would find their way through the vents sooner or later.

Kasai clenched her jaw, shoving the grief aside as she scanned their new surroundings. They were in what looked like an old gym storage room. Faded banners hung limply from the ceiling, and the air was thick with dust and the faint, acrid scent of mildew. Old sports equipment was piled in the corners—deflated basketballs, rusted baseball bats, and a toppled rack of metal lockers that had seen better days.

Milo was still staring at the vent, his face pale and his eyes wide with shock. His shoulders trembled, and his breath came in short, ragged gasps. Elara reached out, placing a firm hand on his shoulder.

"Milo," she said gently but firmly. "We have to go."

Milo shook his head, his voice a hoarse whisper. "We... we left him. We left him."

Kasai knelt down beside him, gripping her wrench tightly in one hand while placing the other on his arm. "I know," she whispered. "But Kyle... he gave us a chance. We can't waste it."

Milo's eyes met hers, and for a moment, Kasai saw the fear and anger swirling in his gaze. But then he nodded, swallowing hard as he forced himself to his feet.

Elara gave Kasai a small, appreciative nod before turning her attention to the room. "We need to find another exit. We can't stay here."

Kasai stood, her legs feeling like lead as she moved toward the far wall, where a door stood partially ajar. She pushed it open cautiously, her flashlight beam cutting through the darkness. Beyond the door was a narrow hallway, lined with cracked tiles and old lockers.

"It looks clear," she whispered, glancing back at the others.

They moved quickly, slipping through the door and into the hallway. The school was eerily silent now, the chaos from earlier replaced by a heavy, oppressive stillness. But Kasai knew better than to trust the quiet. The infected were out there, lurking in the shadows, waiting for the next chance to strike.

As they crept down the hall, Kasai's mind raced. They needed a plan. The school was a death trap—too many blind corners, too many places for the infected to hide. But where else could they go?

Her thoughts were interrupted by a sudden noise—a faint, rhythmic tapping echoing down the corridor. Kasai froze, her heart pounding in her chest as she strained to listen.

Tap. Tap. Tap.

It was coming from one of the classrooms ahead.

Kasai exchanged a tense glance with Elara and Milo. They couldn't afford to ignore it. It could be another survivor—or it could be something much worse.

Gripping her wrench tighter, Kasai moved forward, her footsteps silent on the cracked tiles. She reached the door and pressed her ear against it, listening intently.

Tap. Tap. Tap.

It was slower now, more deliberate. Like someone—or something—was waiting.

Kasai took a deep breath and nodded to Elara, who positioned herself beside the door with her screwdriver raised. Milo hovered behind them, clutching a rusted baseball bat he'd grabbed from the storage room.

Kasai counted down silently—three, two, one—before yanking the door open and raising her wrench, ready to strike.

But what she saw stopped her cold.

It wasn't infected. It was a girl.

She couldn't have been much older than Kasai, her clothes torn and stained with blood, her face pale and gaunt. She was sitting on the floor near the window, tapping a broken piece of glass against the wall in a slow, hypnotic rhythm.

Her eyes snapped up to meet Kasai's, and for a moment, they stared at each other in stunned silence.

Then the girl spoke, her voice hoarse and raspy. "Are you real?"

Kasai lowered her wrench slightly, her heart still racing. "Yeah," she whispered. "We're real. Are you okay?"

The girl let out a shaky laugh, dropping the piece of glass with a soft clink. "Do I look okay?" she muttered, pushing herself to her feet.

Elara stepped forward cautiously, her eyes scanning the girl for any signs of infection. "Are you hurt?"

The girl shook her head, though her movements were stiff and hesitant. "No bites," she said quickly as if she'd had to defend herself before. "I'm clean."

Kasai felt a wave of relief wash over her, but it was quickly replaced by suspicion. "What are you doing here?"

The girl's expression darkened. "Same as you, I guess. Trying not to die."

Milo stepped forward, his voice still shaky. "What's your name?"

The girl hesitated as if weighing whether or not to trust them. Finally, she sighed. "Riley."

Kasai nodded, her grip on the wrench relaxing slightly. "I'm Kasai. This is Elara and Milo."

Riley's eyes flicked to each of them, lingering on the bloodstains and makeshift weapons. "You've been through hell too, huh?"

Kasai let out a bitter laugh. "You could say that."

For a moment, there was silence. Then Elara spoke, her voice gentle but firm. "We need to get out of here. It's not safe."

Riley nodded, her expression hardening. "Yeah. I know a way out."

Kasai's heart leaped. "You do?"

Riley motioned toward the window, where a fire escape ladder was barely visible through the grime-streaked glass. "I was gonna try it before you showed up. It's risky, but it's better than staying here."

Kasai exchanged a glance with Elara and Milo. They didn't have any better options.

"Let's do it," Elara said.

Riley moved to the window, prying it open with a grunt. The cool night air rushed in, carrying with it the distant sounds of sirens and screams. Kasai felt a shiver run down her spine, but she pushed the fear aside.

One by one, they climbed out onto the fire escape, the metal groaning under their weight. The city stretched out below them, a sprawling wasteland of broken buildings and burning cars.

But Kasai didn't focus on the destruction. She focused on survival.

As they descended the ladder, Kasai felt a strange sense of determination settle over her. They had lost Kyle, and they were still in danger. But they weren't alone anymore.

And as long as they kept moving, they had a chance.

A chance to survive the next 70 hours.

The metal rungs of the fire escape groaned under their combined weight, each step a reminder of how fragile their grip on survival was. Kasai's palms were slick with sweat as she carefully descended, her wrench tucked into her belt for quick access. Below her, Milo was already on the ground, scanning the dark alley with wide, jittery eyes, while Elara followed just above, her movements steady despite the tension in the air. Riley brought up the rear, her lean frame navigating the ladder with surprising agility.

The city felt different down here. On the rooftop, they'd had space, a vantage point to see what was coming. Down in the alley, the world closed in, shadows pooling in every corner, hiding threats they couldn't anticipate. The faint orange glow of fires still burning in the distance cast eerie, flickering patterns on the walls, but it did little to push back the suffocating darkness.

Kasai hit the ground softly, crouching next to Milo. His face was pale, and his hands trembled as he clutched the rusted baseball bat tighter than necessary. The loss of Kyle weighed heavily on all of them, but it seemed to hit Milo the hardest.Kasai wanted to say something, anything to reassure him, but the words felt hollow before they even formed.

Elara touched down next, her screwdriver still in hand, and Riley followed moments later, pulling the fire escape ladder up behind her with a grunt. "No point leaving them an easy way down," she muttered, her voice low but sharp.

Kasai gave a tight nod. "Where to now?"

Riley scanned the alley, her sharp eyes flicking from one shadowed corner to the next. "There's an old delivery entrance around the block. Leads into the maintenance tunnels under the city. Not exactly safe, but safer than staying on the streets."

Milo's voice wavered. "More tunnels? We barely made it out of the last one alive."

Kasai glanced at him, her voice steady despite the fear coiling in her stomach. "It's better than being out in the open. We move fast, stick together, and we'll make it."

Elara nodded in agreement, her calm presence grounding them all. "Let's go before we attract more attention."

They crept down the alley, the only sounds of their soft footsteps and the distant wails of the infected somewhere deeper in the city. Every corner they turned felt like another gamble, but the streets were eerily quiet, the chaos having moved elsewhere— for now.

The delivery entrance was exactly where Riley said it would be, tucked behind an abandoned diner with shattered windows and a flickering neon sign that buzzed weakly in the silence. The metal door was dented and rusted, but still intact. Riley approached it cautiously, pulling a bobby pin from her pocket.

Kasai raised an eyebrow. "You know how to pick locks?"

Riley shot her a quick grin, the first sign of lightness Kasai had seen in her. "You pick up a few skills when you've been on your own for a while."

The grin faded almost as quickly as it appeared, replaced by the same guarded look Kasai had seen when they first met. Riley worked quickly, the soft click of tumblers falling into place sounding louder in the quiet.

"Got it," she whispered, pushing the door open with a creak.

The smell hit them immediately—a mix of mildew, rust, and something else. Something rotting. Kasai's stomach churned, but she forced herself to step inside, her flashlight cutting through the gloom.

The tunnel stretched ahead, lined with old, corroded pipes that dripped water onto the cracked concrete floor. The walls were covered in grime and graffiti, messages left by people who probably hadn't made it out. Kasai caught glimpses of them in the flickering light—"HELP US," "THEY'RE EVERYWHERE," and, most chillingly, "NO ONE IS COMING."

Elara moved to the front, her steady gaze scanning the darkness. "Keep your eyes open. These tunnels could be crawling with infected."

They moved cautiously, their footsteps echoing off the walls despite their efforts to stay silent. The deeper they went, the heavier the air felt, thick with moisture and the unmistakable stench of decay. Kasai's grip tightened on her wrench, her heart pounding in her chest.

Milo whispered from behind, his voice barely audible. "How do we even know these tunnels lead anywhere safe?"

Riley glanced over her shoulder, her expression grim. "We don't. But it's better than sitting around waiting to get eaten."

They continued deeper, the tunnel branching off in multiple

directions. Riley seemed to know where she was going, though, leading them down a narrow side passage that sloped downward. The air grew colder, and Kasai could hear something—dripping water, but also something else. A faint, rhythmic sound, like breathing.

They rounded a corner and froze.

Ahead, in the dim light, was a cluster of infected. They were huddled together, their bodies swaying slightly as if in some sort of trance. Their skin was pale, stretched tight over their bones, and their mouths hung open, releasing soft, wet gasps.

Kasai's breath caught in her throat. "What are they doing?" she whispered.

Elara's face was pale, her eyes wide. "I don't know. But we need to get past them."

Riley scanned the walls, her sharp eyes landing on a narrow ledge running along the side of the tunnel. "We can climb over. Stay quiet, and they might not notice."

Kasai's heart pounded as she followed Riley to the ledge. It was barely wide enough to stand on, the slick surface making every step a risk. She pressed her back against the cold wall, inching forward as quietly as she could.

Milo followed, his breathing ragged as he tried to keep his balance. Elara brought up the rear, her movements steady but tense.

They were halfway across when it happened.

Milo slipped.

His foot hit a loose piece of rubble, sending it clattering to the floor below. The sound echoed through the tunnel like a gunshot.

The infected snapped out of their trance instantly. Their heads jerked upward in unison, and for a horrifying moment, they were silent, their cloudy eyes locking onto Kasai and the others.

Then they screamed.

It was a sound Kasai would never forget—raw, inhuman, filled with hunger and rage. The infected surged forward, their movements jerky but terrifyingly fast.

"Go!" Riley shouted, her voice breaking the paralysis that had gripped them.

Kasai bolted, her heart pounding as she scrambled along the ledge. The infected were right behind them, their clawed hands swiping at the air, just inches away.

They reached the end of the ledge, where a rusted metal ladder led up to a hatch. Riley was already climbing, her hands moving faster than Kasai thought possible.

Kasai didn't hesitate. She grabbed the ladder, pulling herself up with everything she had. Milo was right behind her, his face pale with terror, and Elara brought up the rear, her screwdriver clutched tightly in one hand.

The infected hit the base of the ladder just as Kasai reached the top. She threw her shoulder into the hatch, forcing it open with a loud clang.

They spilled out into the open air, the sudden brightness blinding after the darkness of the tunnels. Kasai scrambled to her feet, helping Milo and Elara out just as Riley slammed the hatch shut behind them.

They collapsed on the ground, gasping for breath. The city stretched out around them, broken and burning, but for the first time in hours, Kasai felt a flicker of hope.

They'd made it out.

But the clock was still ticking.

70 hours left.

Chapter 3
The Fragile Calm

Kasai's chest heaved as she lay flat on her back, staring up at the sky. The clouds were streaked with smoke, their soft grays blending into the angry orange of distant fires. The world felt like it was smoldering, the city reduced to a patchwork of ruins and ash. Her body ached from head to toe—scraped knees, bruised ribs, and a burning in her arms from climbing that last ladder like her life depended on it. Because it had.

For a moment, she let herself lie there, listening to the chaotic symphony of the city—sirens wailing somewhere far off, glass shattering in the distance, and the faint, ever-present groans of the infected echoing through the streets like a haunting chorus. But above all that, she could hear the frantic beating of her heart, pounding like a war drum in her ears.

They were alive. For now.

Milo was the first to break the silence. He sat up with a groan, wiping the sweat and grime from his face with the sleeve of his shirt. His hands were still trembling, but there was a flicker of relief in his eyes.

"Didn't think we were getting out of there," he muttered, his voice rough and hoarse.

Kasai forced herself to sit up, wincing as her muscles protested. "Yeah," she breathed, glancing around. "But we did."

They were in an abandoned parking lot, bordered by a crumbling brick wall on one side and an overgrown chain-link fence on the other. Rusted cars sat in crooked lines, their windows shattered and their tires slashed. The scent of smoke and gasoline lingered in the air, mingling with the metallic tang of blood that seemed to cling to everything now.

Elara was already on her feet, her eyes scanning the perimeter with that calm, calculating look Kasai had come to rely on. She looked exhausted—they all did—but there was a steadiness in her posture, a quiet resilience that made Kasai feel a little less like the world was falling apart.

Riley, on the other hand, was pacing near the edge of the lot, her arms crossed tightly over her chest. Her sharp eyes flicked from shadow to shadow, like she was expecting the infected to come bursting out at any moment.

"They'll be looking for us," she said quietly, more to herself than anyone else. "We didn't exactly sneak out of there."

Kasai nodded, dragging her eyes away from the horizon. "We need to move. Find somewhere to rest before nightfall."

Elara turned to face them, her expression serious but calm. "We won't get far if we don't rest first. We've been running non-stop, and we're all exhausted."

Milo let out a bitter laugh. "Rest? Where? There's nowhere safe."

"There's somewhere," Kasai said, forcing more confidence into her voice than she felt. "There has to be."

Riley finally stopped pacing, her eyes narrowing as she studied Kasai. "You keep saying that. Like believing it hard enough will make it true."

Kasai met her gaze, refusing to back down. "Because if I don't believe it, we're already dead."

The words hung in the air for a moment, heavy and unspoken. No one argued because they all knew it was true. Hope was the only thing keeping them going, as fragile as it was.

Elara broke the silence, her voice steady. "There's a library a few blocks from here. Big, old building with thick walls. It might be abandoned, and even if it's not, we'll have cover."

Kasai nodded, grateful for the direction. "Then that's where we're going."

They gathered their things—what little they had left—and started moving. Kasai could feel the exhaustion in her bones, every step heavier than the last, but she pushed forward. One foot in front of the other. That was all she could do.

The streets were eerily quiet as they navigated the maze of debris and destruction. Abandoned cars sat at odd angles, some still smoldering from whatever chaos had unfolded here. Storefronts were shattered, their windows broken like jagged teeth, and graffiti covered the walls—messages scrawled in haste by people who were probably long gone.

"RUN."

"TRUST NO ONE."

"THEY'RE EVERYWHERE."

Kasai tried not to look too closely at the dark stains on the pavement.

They kept to the shadows, ducking behind cars and slipping through alleyways. Every sound made Kasai's heart leap—every distant scream, every rustle of movement in the periphery. The city felt alive, but in the worst way, like it was watching them, waiting for them to slip up.

When they finally reached the library, Kasai felt a flicker of cautious relief. It was a large, imposing building, its stone façade cracked but still standing strong. Tall windows lined the front, most of them shattered, but the heavy wooden doors remained intact.

They approached cautiously, weapons drawn, ready for anything. Kasai's heart pounded as she pushed the door open, the old hinges creaking loudly in the silence.

Inside, the air was cool and still, thick with the scent of dust and old paper. The tall shelves loomed like silent sentinels, casting long shadows across the floor. The grand staircase in the center of the room spiraled upward into darkness, and the faint light filtering through the broken windows gave everything a ghostly glow.

They moved through the library in silence, checking each room, each corner, each shadow. But there was no sign of the infected. No sign of anyone.

When they were finally sure the building was empty, Kasai let out a shaky breath, the tension in her shoulders easing just a little.

"This'll work," Elara said quietly, her eyes scanning the room one last time. "We can barricade the doors, stay here for the night."

Milo collapsed onto one of the dusty couches near the back, letting out a long, exhausted sigh. "I don't care if this place falls down around us. I'm not moving for at least an hour."

Kasai let herself smile, just a little. It wasn't much, but it was something.

They set to work barricading the entrances, dragging heavy tables and bookshelves in front of the doors. The process was slow and exhausting, but it gave Kasai something to focus on, something to keep her mind off the weight of everything they'd lost—and everything they still had to face.

When they were finally done, they gathered near the back of the library, where the shadows felt a little less suffocating. Kasai sank to the floor, her back against a cold wall, and let her eyes drift closed for just a moment.

But sleep didn't come. Not really.

Her mind kept replaying Kyle's last moments, the sound of his scream echoing in her head. She could still see his face, the determination in his eyes as he fought to give them a chance. The guilt gnawed at her, a sharp, persistent ache she couldn't shake.

Riley's voice broke through the silence, soft but steady. "He saved us, you know."

Kasai opened her eyes, glancing at Riley. The other girl wasn't looking at her, just staring out at the darkened library, her arms wrapped tightly around her knees.

"I know," Kasai whispered.

They sat in silence for a while, the weight of their losses

settling over them like a heavy blanket. But beneath that weight was something else—a spark of determination, fragile but real.

They'd made it this far.

And they weren't giving up.

Not yet.

Not ever.

The night stretched on, long and dark and filled with the distant sounds of a city falling apart. But inside the library, Kasai felt something she hadn't felt in a long time.

Hope.

Fragile, flickering, but still burning.

And as long as that spark remained, she knew they had a chance.

A chance to survive the next 69 hours.

Kasai woke with a start, her heart hammering in her chest. For a moment, she had no idea where she was—the towering bookshelves looming like silent giants in the darkness, the faint glow of moonlight spilling through the broken windows, casting jagged shadows across the floor.

Then it all came rushing back.

The infected. The tunnels. Kyle.

She swallowed hard, trying to push down the rising tide of panic. The library was quiet, but not in a peaceful way. It was the kind of quiet that made your skin crawl, the kind that pressed in from all sides, making every breath feel heavier.

Kasai sat up slowly, her muscles stiff and sore. She glanced around at the others. Elara was propped against a bookshelf nearby, her eyes closed but her grip still firm on the screwdriver resting in her lap. Milo was curled up on one of the old couches, his chest rising and falling in slow, steady breaths, his rusted baseball bat resting against his leg. Riley was nowhere to be seen.

Kasai's heart skipped a beat. She stood, wincing as her legs protested, and moved quietly through the library, her flashlight casting a soft beam of light that flickered across the walls. She checked the main reading room first—empty.Then the stairwell leads to the second floor. Still no sign of her.

Where the hell did she go?

Kasai felt a knot of worry tighten in her chest as she crept toward the back of the library, where a set of heavy wooden doors led to a courtyard. She pushed one open just enough to slip through, the cool night air washing over her like a wave.

And there, sitting on the edge of a crumbling stone fountain, was Riley.

Kasai let out a breath she hadn't realized she was holding and approached slowly, her footsteps soft on the cracked pavement. Riley didn't turn around. She just stared up at the sky, her arms wrapped around her knees, the moonlight casting a pale glow over her face.

Kasai stopped a few feet away, unsure of what to say. Finally, she settled on, "You okay?"

Riley let out a soft, bitter laugh. "You really think anyone's okay right now?"

Kasai sat down next to her, the cold stone seeping through her jeans. "Fair point."

They sat in silence for a while, the sounds of the city a distant hum—sirens, distant screams, the occasional pop of gunfire echoing through the night. Kasai tried not to think about what was happening out there. She tried to focus on the stars instead, faint and distant against the smoky sky.

After a while, Riley spoke again, her voice softer this time. "I used to come here when I was a kid. This library. My mom would bring me every Saturday."

Kasai glanced at her, surprised. "Really?"

Riley nodded, a small, sad smile tugging at the corners of her mouth. "Yeah. She loved books. Said they were like little escape hatches from the real world." She let out a shaky breath. "Guess we could use one of those now, huh?"

Kasai didn't know what to say to that, so she just nodded, staring down at her hands.

"My mom's gone," Riley said quietly, her voice barely more than a whisper. "She was sick before all this started. Cancer. I was taking care of her when... when everything went to hell." She laughed, but there was no humor in it. "Can you believe that? The world ends, and I'm still stuck in that crappy apartment, watching her die. But it wasn't the cancer that got her."

Kasai felt her stomach twist. She didn't want to hear the rest of the story, but she knew Riley needed to say it.

"She turned," Riley whispered. "Right in front of me. One minute she was my mom, and the next... she was one of them." She shook her head, her eyes shining in the moonlight. "I couldn't do it. I couldn't..." Her voice broke, and she pressed her hands to her face, letting out a ragged sob.

Kasai's heart ached. She didn't know what it felt like to lose a parent that way, but she knew what it felt like to lose someone. She reached out, placing a hand on Riley's shoulder, offering silent support.

For a long time, they just sat there, the weight of their shared grief filling the space between them.

Finally, Riley wiped her eyes and let out a shaky breath. "Sorry. I didn't mean to dump all that on you."

Kasai shook her head. "It's okay. We've all lost people."

Riley nodded, her gaze distant. "Yeah. But that doesn't make it any easier, does it?"

Kasai didn't have an answer for that. She wasn't sure anyone did.

They sat in silence for a while longer before Riley finally stood, brushing the dirt from her jeans. "We should get back. Before Milo wakes up and has a panic attack."

Kasai managed a small smile and followed her back into the library.

Inside, the others were still asleep, the faint glow of dawn just beginning to creep through the broken windows. Kasai settled back against the wall, exhaustion pulling at her, but sleep didn't come. She just stared out at the slowly brightening sky, her mind racing with thoughts of what lay ahead.

They had made it through another night. But the sun rising didn't mean they were safe.

It just meant they had survived another day.

68 hours left.

The sun crept through the shattered windows of the library, casting jagged lines of light across the dusty floor. The soft, golden hue seemed out of place against the backdrop of their ragged breathing, bruised skin, and the overwhelming weight of survival. Morning didn't bring peace—it only reminded them that the clock was still ticking.

Kasai stretched her sore limbs, wincing as her muscles protested. She'd managed maybe an hour of sleep, but her mind had stayed restless, haunted by memories of Kyle's last scream and the infected's relentless chase through the tunnels. She rubbed her eyes, trying to push away the exhaustion threatening to drag her down.

Milo stirred on the couch, his face pale and his dark hair sticking to his forehead with sweat. He blinked up at the broken ceiling, disoriented for a moment before reality crashed back in. Kasai watched as the hope faded from his expression, replaced by the same grim determination they all wore like armor.

"Morning," she murmured, her voice hoarse from disuse.

Milo let out a humorless laugh. "Morning. Like that means anything anymore."

Kasai didn't argue. He was right. Time had lost its meaning. Daylight didn't promise safety, and nighttime wasn't the only thing to fear. The infected didn't care if it was dawn or dusk. They just were.

Elara woke next, pushing herself up from her spot against the bookshelf with a quiet groan. Despite the exhaustion written across her face, she moved with a kind of calm efficiency that Kasai had come to expect. It was like she had an endless reserve of strength tucked away, and Kasai was grateful for it.

Riley joined them shortly after, her expression guarded as she stepped into the faint morning light. The conversation they'd shared the night before lingered between them, unspoken but understood. Kasai offered a small nod, and Riley returned it, the brief exchange enough to solidify the fragile trust growing between them.

Elara clapped her hands softly, drawing their attention. "We need to figure out our next move."

Kasai sighed, rubbing the back of her neck. "We can't stay here. The library's too exposed. If the infected don't find us, other people might."

Riley nodded in agreement. "Yeah. And not everyone out there's just trying to survive. Some people..." She trailed off, her eyes darkening with a memory she didn't share.

Milo shivered, hugging his arms to his chest. "So, what then? Where do we go?"

Elara pulled out a rough map of the city she'd found tucked inside one of the library's desks. She spread it out on the floor, weighing down the corners with random objects—an old book, a broken flashlight, a can of food they'd managed to scavenge.

"There's a community center a few miles from here," Elara said, pointing to a spot on the map. "Big place, used to run emergency drills. If anyone's still organizing survivors, they might be there."

Kasai studied the map, her stomach twisting with both hope and dread. A part of her wanted to believe there was still some kind of structure out there, someone trying to help. But another part—the louder part—knew better. They couldn't rely on anyone but themselves.

"Alright," she said finally. "We head for the community center. But we do it carefully. We can't risk running into another horde."

Milo groaned softly, looking out one of the broken windows at the ruined streets below. "A few miles might as well be a hundred with those things out there."

Riley snorted. "Better start walking then."

They packed their things quickly, stuffing what little supplies they had into their worn-out backpacks. Kasai adjusted the strap on her shoulder, feeling the comforting weight of her wrench against her side. It wasn't much, but it had saved her life more than once.

Before they left, Elara paused at the entrance of the library, her eyes scanning the dusty shelves one last time. Kasai watched her, curious.

"You good?" Kasai asked quietly.

Elara nodded slowly but didn't turn around. "Just... remembering."

Kasai didn't push. They all had memories tied to places like this—places that had once felt safe, and normal. But those places didn't exist anymore. The world had changed, and they had to change with it.

They stepped out into the morning light, the city spread before them like a battlefield. The streets were eerily quiet, the usual hum of life replaced by a heavy silence that pressed down on them like a weight.

Kasai took the lead, her eyes scanning every shadow, every broken window, every overturned car. The others followed close behind, their footsteps soft against the cracked pavement.

The first few blocks were mercifully clear, but Kasai knew better than to trust the calm. The infected could be anywhere—hiding in buildings, lurking around corners, waiting for the perfect moment to strike.

They moved quickly, sticking to alleyways and side streets, avoiding the main roads where the infected were more likely to roam. The city felt like a graveyard, the remnants of its former life scattered like debris around them.

A rusted bicycle lay abandoned on the sidewalk, its wheels still spinning lazily in the breeze. A stroller tipped over near a shattered storefront, its contents—tiny clothes, a stuffed animal—spilled across the ground like an offering.

Kasai forced herself to look away, focusing instead on the path ahead. She couldn't afford to dwell on what had been lost. Not now.

They were halfway to the community center when they heard it—a faint, rhythmic thumping echoing through the empty streets.

Kasai froze, her heart leaping into her throat. She motioned for the others to stop, her eyes scanning the area for the source of the sound.

It was coming from an alley up ahead, just around the corner.

Riley crept forward, her steps silent, and peeked around the edge of the building. She tensed immediately, her face going pale.

Kasai moved to her side, her breath catching in her throat at what she saw.

A group of infected—at least ten of them—were huddled in the alley, their bodies swaying in that eerie, trance-like rhythm Kasai had seen before. But this time, something was different.

They weren't just standing there. They were feeding.

A man lay sprawled on the ground beneath them, his body torn and bloodied, but his eyes were still open, still aware. His mouth moved silently, forming words Kasai couldn't hear.

She felt bile rise in her throat, but she forced it down. They couldn't help him. And if they tried, they'd be dead in seconds.

She pulled back from the corner, her heart pounding in her chest. "We need to go. Now."

The others didn't argue. They turned and started back the way they came, but they hadn't taken more than a few steps when Milo tripped over a loose piece of debris, his foot catching on a rusted pipe.

The sound echoed through the alley like a gunshot.

Kasai's heart stopped.

The infected froze, their heads snapping up in unison. For a heartbeat, the world was silent.

Then they screamed.

Kasai grabbed Milo's arm, yanking him to his feet. "Run!" she shouted, her voice hoarse with panic.

They bolted down the street, their footsteps pounding against the pavement. The infected were right behind them, their snarls and shrieks echoing through the empty streets like a nightmare come to life.

Kasai's lungs burned as she pushed herself harder, her legs screaming in protest. They needed to find cover—now.

Riley spotted an old storefront up ahead, its door hanging open. "In there!" she shouted, veering toward it.

They dove inside, slamming the door shut behind them. Elara and Kasai grabbed a nearby shelf, shoving it against the door just as the infected slammed into it from the other side.

The entire building shook under the force of their assault, the glass windows rattling in their frames.

Kasai's heart pounded in her chest as she pressed her back against the door, her breath coming in ragged gasps.

They weren't safe. Not yet.
But they were still alive.
And that was enough.
For now.

67 hours left.

The door trembled under the weight of the infected slamming against it. Kasai pressed her shoulder into the makeshift barricade of shelves, her muscles screaming as she tried to hold it in place. She could hear them on the other side—snarling, clawing, the sickening scrape of nails against the wood, and the wet slap of bodies hurling themselves forward in blind hunger.

Milo was on the floor, gasping for breath, his face pale as he stared at the door like it might burst open at any second. Riley had already pulled him to his feet, shoving a rusted metal rod into his hands. "If they get in, you swing," she hissed, her voice sharp with urgency.

Elara was the only one still calm, her eyes scanning the room for anything they could use to reinforce the door. She found a length of metal piping and wedged it between the shelf and the floor, creating an improvised brace.

But it wouldn't hold forever.

Kasai could feel the weight of every second pressing down on her. They were trapped in an old hardware store, the kind with dusty shelves and flickering fluorescent lights, the kind that smelled like rust and old wood. The irony wasn't lost on her— they were surrounded by tools and supplies, but none of it mattered if they couldn't keep the infected out.

The pounding at the door grew more frantic, more desperate as if the creatures could smell their fear through the cracks.

"We can't stay here!" Kasai shouted over the noise, her breath coming in ragged gasps.

"No shit!" Milo snapped, his voice high with panic.

"There's a back room!" Elara called, pointing to a narrow hallway at the rear of the store. "If we can get through, there might be a loading dock or a window we can escape from."

Kasai didn't hesitate. "Go! I'll hold this as long as I can."

Riley grabbed Milo by the arm, dragging him toward the back

room. Elara followed close behind, pausing just long enough to press a reassuring hand to Kasai's shoulder.

"You don't have to be a hero," she said quietly.

Kasai gave her a grim smile. "I'm not. I just don't want to be lunch."

Elara disappeared into the hallway, and Kasai was alone with the sounds of the infected. She could feel the barricade giving way, the wood creaking and groaning under the relentless assault.

With a final, bone-deep breath, Kasai shoved herself away from the door and sprinted toward the back of the store. She barely made it five steps before the door splintered behind her, the shelf crashing to the floor as the infected poured in.

Kasai didn't look back. She couldn't look back. She focused on the hallway ahead, on the faint sound of Elara's voice calling her name.

She burst into the back room, slamming the door shut behind her and throwing the bolt into place. But it was flimsy—just a thin piece of metal that wouldn't hold for more than a few seconds.

Elara was already prying open a rusted metal door on the far side of the room, her hands slick with sweat and grime. Riley was stacking boxes in front of the windows, trying to block any potential entry points, while Milo fumbled with a crowbar, his hands shaking too badly to get a good grip.

"Kasai, help me!" Elara shouted, her voice strained.

Kasai crossed the room in two steps, grabbing the edge of the metal door and pulling with everything she had. The rusted hinges groaned in protest, but the door finally gave way, swinging open to reveal a narrow alley bathed in harsh sunlight.

"Go!" Elara ordered, shoving Milo through the doorway first. Riley followed, her eyes flicking nervously over her shoulder as the infected pounded against the back room door.

Kasai and Elara were the last to leave, slamming the metal door shut behind them just as the infected broke through the flimsy barrier inside.

They didn't wait to see if the creatures would follow. They ran.

The alley was narrow and choked with debris—overturned dumpsters, broken pallets, and shattered glass that crunched under their feet as they sprinted toward the street. Kasai's lungs burned, and her legs felt like lead, but she didn't slow down. She couldn't slow down.

They burst out onto a side street, the sudden brightness of the sun blinding after the dimness of the store. For a moment, Kasai thought they were safe.

Then she saw them.

A second group of infected, drawn by the noise, was already barreling down the street toward them.

Kasai's heart sank. There were too many. They'd never outrun them.

But Riley didn't hesitate. She grabbed Kasai's arm and yanked her toward a nearby building—an old apartment complex with boarded-up windows and a rusted fire escape hanging precariously from the side.

"This way!" Riley shouted, already scrambling up the metal ladder.

Kasai followed the others close behind. The infected were right on their heels, their snarls echoing through the empty streets as they clawed at the base of the fire escape.

The metal groaned under their combined weight as they climbed, the rusted bolts creaking ominously with every step. Kasai's heart pounded in her chest, fear and adrenaline driving her upward.

They reached the roof just as the infected started climbing after them, their clawed hands scraping against the metal ladder with a sickening sound.

Kasai didn't stop to think. She grabbed a loose brick from the rooftop and hurled it at the ladder, striking one of the rusted bolts. The metal gave way with a loud clang, and the ladder collapsed, taking the infected with it.

They hit the ground with a sickening thud, but it wouldn't be long before they found another way up.

Kasai staggered back from the edge, her chest heaving as she tried to catch her breath. The city stretched out around them, broken and burning, but for the first time in hours, they had a moment of respite.

They were alive.

For now.

Riley collapsed onto the roof, her breath coming in ragged gasps. "That was way too close."

Milo sank down next to her, his face pale and his eyes wide with shock. "We're gonna die out here," he whispered, his voice trembling. "There's no way we're gonna make it."

Kasai shook her head, forcing herself to stand. "We're not dead yet. As long as we keep moving, we have a chance."

Elara nodded, her face calm despite the chaos they'd just escaped. "We'll rest here for a bit, then figure out our next move."

Kasai turned to look out over the city, her heart still pounding in her chest. The infected were everywhere. The streets below teemed with them, their twisted forms moving like shadows through the ruins of what had once been a thriving city.

But Kasai wasn't ready to give up. Not yet.

They had survived another attack, another brush with death.

And as long as they were still breathing, they had a chance.

A chance to survive the next 66 hours.

Kasai's muscles burned as she paced the rooftop, her heart still pounding in her chest. The city stretched out below them, a patchwork of collapsed buildings overturned cars, and trails of smoke rising into the sky like warning flares. She could hear the infected below—low, guttural growls, punctuated by the occasional shriek as they prowled the streets, searching for their next victim.

But up here, for the first time in what felt like days, there was silence.

Not the kind of silence that came with danger lurking just around the corner, but a fragile, delicate quiet that Kasai clung to like a lifeline. She let herself breathe, just for a moment.

Behind her, Milo sat slumped against an old ventilation unit, his chest rising and falling in slow, uneven breaths. His face was pale, streaked with grime and sweat, but his eyes were wide open, staring at the sky like he'd forgotten what it looked like.

Riley leaned against the rusted railing at the edge of the roof, arms crossed tightly over her chest. The wind tugged at her hair, and though her face was calm, Kasai could see the tension in her jaw, the slight tremble in her fingers.

Elara was the only one moving with purpose. She crouched near the stairwell entrance, examining the rusted hatch that led back down into the building. Her calm, steady presence grounded them all, but even Kasai could see the exhaustion in her shoulders, the way her hands trembled just slightly when she thought no one was looking.

Kasai finally stopped pacing, running a hand through her tangled hair. "We can't stay up here forever," she said quietly, her voice hoarse from exhaustion. "We need to figure out our next move."

Riley let out a bitter laugh, shaking her head. "What next move? We've been running since this started. How much longer do you think we can keep this up?"

Kasai met her gaze, refusing to let the fear take over. "As long as it takes."

Milo let out a shaky breath, his voice barely a whisper. "I don't know if I can do this anymore."

Elara finally stood, wiping her hands on her pants as she crossed the rooftop to join them. "You can," she said firmly, her voice steady and calm. "We all can. We don't have a choice."

Kasai nodded, feeling the weight of Elara's words settle over her like a heavy blanket. They didn't have a choice. Giving up wasn't an option. Not if they wanted to survive.

She took a deep breath, forcing herself to focus. "The community center is still our best bet. It's only a few miles from here. If we move fast, we can make it before dark."

Riley frowned, her arms still crossed tightly over her chest. "And what if it's crawling with those things? What if there's nothing there?"

Kasai didn't have an answer for that. But she knew they couldn't stay here. Not with the infected swarming the streets below.

"We have to try," she said finally, her voice quiet but firm.

"It's better than sitting up here waiting to die."

Elara nodded in agreement. "We'll rest for a little while, then we'll move. We can't afford to waste time."

The others didn't argue. They knew she was right.

Kasai sank to the ground, leaning back against the cool metal of the ventilation unit. She closed her eyes, letting the wind wash over her, trying to ignore the ache in her muscles, the exhaustion pulling at her like a tide.

But sleep didn't come.

Her mind raced with memories—Kyle's scream, the infected's snarls, the feel of her mother's last text burning in her pocket. "Lock the doors. Don't let anyone in. I love you."

She clenched her jaw, forcing the memories down. She couldn't afford to dwell on the past. Not now.

When the sun began to dip below the horizon, painting the sky in shades of orange and pink, Elara stood, brushing the dust from her pants.

"It's time," she said quietly.

Kasai pushed herself to her feet, her body protesting with every movement. But she ignored the pain. They had to move.

Riley led the way to the fire escape, her movements cautious but determined. Milo followed, his grip tight on the rusted baseball bat, his face pale but set with grim determination.

Kasai took one last look at the city before climbing down after them, the cool metal of the ladder biting into her palms.

They moved through the streets like shadows, sticking to the alleys and side streets, avoiding the main roads where the infected were more likely to be. The city felt like a graveyard, the remnants of its former life scattered like debris around them.

They passed an overturned car, its windows shattered, and Kasai caught a glimpse of a family photo lying on the ground—a mother, a father, and two kids smiling brightly at the camera. She forced herself to look away, focusing instead on the path ahead.

They were halfway to the community center when they heard it—a faint, rhythmic thumping echoing through the empty streets.

Kasai froze, her heart leaping into her throat. She motioned for the others to stop, her eyes scanning the area for the source of the sound.

It was coming from a nearby building, the soft, steady beat of something—or someone—moving inside.

Riley crept forward, her steps silent, and peeked through a broken window. She tensed immediately, her face going pale.

Kasai moved to her side, her breath catching in her throat at what she saw.

It wasn't infected. It was people.

A group of survivors huddled in the corner of the building, their faces gaunt and hollow, their clothes torn and stained with blood. But there was something wrong about them—something in the way they moved, the way their eyes flicked nervously around the room as if they were expecting something—or someone—to find them.

Kasai felt a knot of unease tighten in her chest.

"We should keep moving," she whispered, pulling Riley back from the window.

But before they could retreat, a voice rang out from inside the building.

"Hey! Over here!"

Kasai's heart dropped. One of the survivors had seen them.

The others in the group scrambled to their feet, their faces lighting up with a mix of hope and desperation as they stumbled toward the door.

Kasai turned to the others, her mind racing. They couldn't just leave them. But they couldn't risk getting trapped, either.

Elara stepped forward, her voice calm but firm. "We help them. But we do it carefully."

Kasai nodded, tightening her grip on her wrench. They didn't have a choice.

As they approached the building, the survivors poured out onto the street, their faces alight with relief.

But that relief was short-lived.

The infected had heard the commotion.

Kasai could hear them coming—their snarls and shrieks echoing through the empty streets like a nightmare come to life.

She didn't have time to think. She grabbed the nearest survivor, pulling them toward the alley.

"Run!" she shouted, her voice hoarse with panic.

They sprinted down the street, the infected hot on their heels. Kasai's lungs burned, her legs screaming in protest, but she didn't stop. She couldn't stop.

They rounded a corner, diving into an abandoned storefront, slamming the door shut behind them.

Kasai pressed her back against the door, her chest heaving as the infected pounded against the other side.

They weren't safe. Not yet.

But they were still alive.

And that was enough.

For now.

65 hours left.

Chapter 4
No Safe Havens

Kasai pressed her back against the door, the vibrations from the infected pounding against it reverberating through her spine. The snarls and guttural growls on the other side were relentless, a reminder that death was always just a few inches of wood away. Her chest heaved with every breath, lungs burning from the sprint through the streets. She could feel the fear simmering beneath her skin, but she shoved it down. Fear wouldn't keep them alive.

The room they'd stumbled into was dark and musty, filled with broken shelves and overturned tables. The air smelled like mildew and rust, the remnants of whatever this place used to be lost beneath layers of dust and decay. Kasai could hear the others behind her—Elara's steady breathing, Milo's ragged gasps, Riley's soft curses as she checked the barricades.

But it was the strangers—the survivors they'd just risked everything to save—that Kasai focused on now.

There were five of them, huddled together in the corner of the room like frightened animals. Their faces were pale, their eyes wide with a mixture of fear and disbelief. They looked more like ghosts than people, their clothes torn and stained, their bodies thin from starvation or worse.

One of them—a man with a patchy beard and hollow eyes—stepped forward, his hands raised in a gesture of peace. "Thank you," he rasped, his voice raw and strained. "We... we didn't think anyone else was out here."

Kasai nodded, though she wasn't sure if she felt relief or regret. Helping them had been a gut decision, but now that they were trapped together, she wasn't sure if it had been the right one.

Elara took a step closer to Kasai, her voice low and steady. "We can't stay here long. The door won't hold forever."

Kasai nodded, her mind already racing for solutions. They needed a way out, but the streets were crawling with infected, and their supplies were running dangerously low.

Riley moved to the boarded-up window, peering through a crack in the wood. "There's an alley behind this building," she whispered. "It's narrow. If we move fast, we might lose them."

Kasai turned back to the strangers, her gaze hardening. "Can you run?"

The man with the beard nodded quickly. "We can. We're not... we're not injured or anything."

Kasai didn't have time to question that. She just hoped they were telling the truth.

"Alright," she said, turning back to the group. "We're moving out the back. Stay quiet, stay close, and don't stop for anything."

Milo let out a shaky breath, his grip tightening on the rusted baseball bat in his hands. "We're gonna die," he muttered, more to himself than anyone else.

Kasai shot him a look. "Not if we move fast."

Elara moved to the window, pulling a crowbar from her belt and prying the boards loose with careful, practiced movements. The wood groaned softly, but the sounds of the infected pounding on the door drowned out the noise.

When the boards finally gave way, Kasai was the first through the window, dropping into the alley below. The air outside was cold and sharp, filled with the distant sounds of chaos—the screams of the infected, the occasional crack of gunfire from somewhere far off.

She scanned the alley quickly. It was narrow, the walls on either side closing in like a tunnel. But it was empty. For now.

She turned back to the window. "Come on!"

One by one, the others climbed through the window, landing softly on the cracked pavement. Elara was the last to drop down, her eyes scanning the shadows as she joined them.

They didn't wait. Kasai led the way down the alley, her heart pounding in her chest. Every step felt like a countdown, every corner a gamble. She could hear the infected behind them, their snarls growing fainter as they moved deeper into the maze of backstreets.

But Kasai knew better than to think they were safe.

They weren't safe. Not anywhere.

After what felt like hours, they finally slowed, ducking into a small, abandoned shop to catch their breath. Kasai collapsed against the wall, her chest heaving as she tried to calm her racing heart.

The strangers were huddled together in the corner, whispering among themselves. Kasai watched them closely, her instincts on high alert. She didn't know them. She didn't trust them. But they were here now, and that meant they were part of the equation.

Elara moved to Kasai's side, her voice low and quiet. "We need to figure out who they are. We can't afford any surprises."

Kasai nodded. She pushed herself to her feet, crossing the room to where the man with the beard was sitting.

"What's your name?" she asked her voice firm but not unkind.

The man looked up at her, his eyes wary. "Caleb," he said after a moment. "My name's Caleb." He gestured to the others in the group—a woman with dark hair and a haunted expression, a teenage boy who couldn't have been older than sixteen, and two younger girls clinging to each other like their lives depended on it. "That's Sarah, Jason, and the girls are Emma and Lucy."

Kasai studied them for a moment, trying to gauge if they were a threat. They didn't *look* dangerous—just scared and desperate. But Kasai knew better than to trust appearances.

"Where were you headed?" she asked, her eyes narrowing slightly.

Caleb swallowed hard, glancing at his group before answering. "We were trying to get to the evacuation point. We heard there was a safe zone near the river."

Kasai felt her stomach twist. She'd heard those rumors too. But so far, they'd found nothing but death and destruction.

"There's no safe zone," she said quietly. "Not that we've seen."

Caleb's face fell, the hope draining from his eyes. The others in his group looked just as shattered, their shoulders slumping as the reality of their situation sank in.

Kasai felt a pang of guilt, but she shoved it down. False hope wouldn't keep them alive.

"We're heading to the community center," she continued. "If anyone's still organizing survivors, that's where they'll be."

Caleb nodded slowly. "Then we'll come with you."

Kasai didn't argue. They were stronger in numbers, even if it meant more mouths to feed and more people to protect.

"We'll rest here for a bit," she said, turning back to the group. "Then we move."

The others nodded, settling into uneasy silence. Kasai sank back against the wall, her mind racing. The clock was still ticking, and they were running out of time.

But for now, they were alive.

And that was enough.

64 hours left.

The shadows stretched longer as the sun dipped lower, casting an eerie orange glow through the cracked windows of the abandoned shop. Dust floated in the air, illuminated by the fading light, and the once-quiet hum of the city had shifted into something darker—more sinister. The distant screams were becoming more frequent, and every distant crash sounded like it was getting closer.

Kasai sat near the entrance, her back against the cold wall, fingers absently tracing the chipped edge of her wrench. She could hear the others shifting restlessly behind her. Milo muttered to himself as he fiddled with the rusted baseball bat, while Riley paced in tight circles, her eyes darting to the windows every few seconds. Elara sat quietly, sharpening a piece of metal she'd fashioned into a makeshift blade. She was the only one who seemed to carry the weight of what they'd just survived with an unsettling calmness.

The group they'd rescued huddled together in the far corner, whispering among themselves. Kasai watched them from the corner of her eye. Caleb, the man with the patchy beard, kept glancing toward Kasai like he wanted to say something but couldn't find the courage to speak. His group—Sarah, Jason, and the two younger girls, Emma and Lucy—looked even more fragile up close. The girls were clinging to each other, their faces pale, eyes too wide for kids their age. Jason, the teenager, had that same haunted look Milo sometimes wore—the kind that said he'd seen more death than anyone his age should.

Finally, Caleb cleared his throat, breaking the tense silence.

"I... I know you didn't have to help us back there," he said, his voice hoarse but steady. "But thank you."

Kasai nodded curtly, not sure how to respond. She hadn't saved them out of kindness. She'd done it because it felt like the right thing to do in that split second. But now, with every heartbeat, she questioned if adding more people to their fragile group had been the smart choice.

"We need to stick together," Elara said quietly, her voice cutting through the tension like a knife. "It's the only way we're going to make it."

Caleb nodded, his eyes flicking between Kasai and Elara. "We'll pull our weight," he promised. "We're not expecting handouts."

Kasai wanted to believe him. But she'd seen how desperation changed people. She'd seen what fear could do, how it twisted good intentions into dangerous choices.

"We're heading to the community center," Kasai said, her voice low but firm. "If there's anyone still out there organizing survivors, that's where they'll be."

Caleb's expression tightened, but he nodded. "We heard about that place, too. But..." He hesitated, his gaze dropping to the floor. "We came from that direction. Didn't see anything that looked like a safe zone. Just more of *them*."

The room fell silent. Kasai felt the familiar pit of dread settle in her stomach, but she refused to let it show.

"We're not dead yet," Riley snapped, breaking the silence. "And until we are, we keep moving."

Milo let out a shaky breath. "Yeah, but for how long? We've been running non-stop. There's gotta be a limit to how long we can keep this up."

Kasai clenched her jaw, forcing down the wave of exhaustion threatening to swallow her whole. Milo was right. They couldn't keep running forever. But they also couldn't afford to stop. Not yet.

"We'll rest here for a little longer," Elara said, standing and slipping her blade into the waistband of her pants. "Then we move. We'll take the back streets, and stay off the main roads. It's slower, but it's safer."

Kasai nodded, grateful for Elara's steady presence. It felt like the only thing holding them together.

As the light outside faded into twilight, Kasai felt the familiar prick of anxiety crawling up her spine. The night was the worst time to be out in the city. The infected were more aggressive and more unpredictable, and the darkness made it impossible to see them coming until it was too late.

But staying put wasn't an option either.

Elara gave them all a nod. "Time to move."

Kasai pushed herself to her feet, wincing as her muscles protested. She adjusted the strap on her backpack, feeling the comforting weight of her wrench resting against her hip. The others followed suit, gathering their makeshift weapons and supplies with quiet determination.

They slipped out of the shop through a back door, the cool night air hitting Kasai like a slap to the face. The streets were bathed in shadows, the flickering light from distant fires casting everything in an eerie, orange glow.

They moved quickly, their footsteps soft against the cracked pavement. Kasai led the way, her eyes scanning every shadow, every broken window, every darkened alley. The city felt like it was holding its breath, waiting for them to slip up.

They were halfway to the community center when they heard it—a soft, shuffling noise echoing from the alley up ahead.

Kasai froze, motioning for the others to stop. She strained her ears, trying to make sense of the sound. It wasn't the frantic, snarling noise of the infected. It was something else.

Elara crept forward, peering around the corner of the building. When she pulled back, her expression was unreadable.

"It's people," she whispered. "Looks like another group of survivors."

"We can't trust them," Riley hissed, her eyes narrowing. "We don't know what they want."

"But they might have supplies," Milo whispered, his voice shaky. "Or information."

Kasai weighed their options. They could try to sneak past and avoid the risk entirely. But if the group saw them first, it could turn into a disaster. Or... they could approach carefully and hope for the best.

She turned to Elara. "We approach slowly. Weapons down, but ready."

Elara nodded. Riley grumbled something under her breath but didn't argue.

They stepped into the alley, their movements cautious. The group of survivors spotted them almost immediately—five men, all armed, their faces hard and unwelcoming.

One of them, a tall man with a scar running down the side of his face, stepped forward. His eyes raked over Kasai and her group, lingering on their weapons.

"You lost?" he asked, his voice low and dangerous.

Kasai swallowed hard, keeping her expression neutral. "We're heading to the community center," she said carefully. "Heard there might be survivors gathering there."

The man snorted, glancing back at his group. "Ain't nothing at that community center but bodies. You're wasting your time."

Kasai felt her stomach twist. "You've been there?"

The man's eyes darkened. "Yeah. The place is crawling with

those things. If you're smart, you'll turn around and head the other way."

Kasai exchanged a glance with Elara. If what this man said was true, their best hope for safety might already be gone. But Kasai didn't trust him. Not completely.

"Thanks for the warning," she said, her voice cool. "But we'll take our chances."

The man's smile was thin and humorless. "Suit yourself."

Kasai motioned for her group to keep moving, her heart pounding in her chest as they passed the strangers. She could feel their eyes on her back, the tension in the air thick enough to cut with a knife.

When they were a safe distance away, Milo let out a shaky breath. "You think they were telling the truth?"

Kasai didn't answer immediately. She wasn't sure. But it didn't matter. They had to see for themselves.

"We'll find out soon enough," she said quietly.

They moved through the night, the city around them feeling more dangerous with every step. The encounter with the strangers had shaken them, but it also steeled their resolve. They couldn't afford to give up hope. Not yet.

As they neared the community center, Kasai felt a flicker of something—hope, maybe, or fear. The building loomed in the distance, its dark silhouette standing out against the flickering fires around it.

They were close now.

But whether they were walking into salvation or another nightmare, Kasai didn't know.

All she knew was that they were still alive.

And that was enough.

63 hours left.

The community center loomed in the distance, its shadowed silhouette against the backdrop of a burning sky. The fires across the city cast an eerie orange glow on the building's facade, making it look less like a place of refuge and more like a forgotten monument in a dying world.

Kasai slowed her pace as they approached, her eyes scanning

the surrounding streets and alleys for any signs of movement. The air was unnervingly still. No snarls, no distant screams, not even the shuffle of the infected. It was the kind of silence that made her skin crawl, the quiet before a storm.

Elara stepped up beside her, her gaze hard and calculating as she examined the darkened windows of the community center. "It's too quiet," she murmured, her voice barely above a whisper.

Riley let out a low curse from behind them. "Places like this? They're either full of bodies or worse. I don't like it."

Milo, gripping his baseball bat so tightly his knuckles turned white, swallowed hard. "What's worse than *them*?"

Riley shot him a grim look. "People."

Kasai didn't disagree. She'd seen what people were capable of when the world started falling apart. Desperation changed them, twisted them into something even more dangerous than the infected. At least with the infected, you knew what you were up against.

But they were here now. And there was no turning back.

"We need to check it out," Kasai said firmly, forcing the unease from her voice. "If there's even a chance someone's in there, we have to know."

Caleb and his group huddled behind them and looked just as wary. The younger girls, Emma and Lucy, clung to Sarah's sides, their wide eyes reflecting the faint glow of the fires. Jason, the teenage boy, kept glancing nervously at the shadows, his fingers twitching near the handle of a small kitchen knife he'd picked up somewhere along the way.

Kasai turned to them. "Stay close. And stay quiet."

The group moved cautiously toward the building, sticking to the shadows and keeping their footsteps light on the cracked pavement. The front doors of the community center were ajar, one of them hanging crookedly from its hinges like it had been forced open. Kasai's stomach tightened.

They slipped inside, the heavy door creaking softly as Kasai pushed it open just enough for them to pass through. The interior was dark, the only light coming from the flickering emergency exit signs and the distant glow from the fires outside.

The lobby was a mess. Chairs overturned, papers scattered across the floor, and dark, dried blood smeared along the walls. The reception desk was empty, the computer monitors shattered and covered in dust.

But there were no bodies.

Kasai's heart pounded in her chest as she scanned the room. The lack of bodies didn't comfort her. If anything, it made her more uneasy. *Where is everyone?*

Elara moved ahead, her makeshift blade drawn as she checked the nearby hallways. Riley covered the opposite side, her sharp eyes darting into every shadow. Kasai motioned for Milo and Caleb's group to stay near the entrance, keeping them within sight in case they needed to bolt.

They moved deeper into the building, the silence pressing down on them like a weight. The fluorescent lights flickered overhead, casting everything in a harsh, intermittent glow.

Kasai pushed open a door to what looked like a cafeteria. The tables were overturned, trays of rotting food still sitting where they'd been abandoned. The smell hit her like a punch to the gut— sour, metallic, and thick with decay.

But again... no bodies.

"This doesn't make sense," Milo whispered, his voice shaking. "Where is everyone?"

Kasai didn't have an answer. But she knew something was very, very wrong.

They regrouped near the gymnasium, the largest room in the center. The heavy double doors were slightly ajar, and a faint, rhythmic sound drifted through the gap.

Kasai motioned for the others to stay back as she approached, her wrench gripped tightly in her hand. She pressed her ear against the door, her heart pounding so loudly she could barely hear anything else.

Then she realized what the sound was.

Breathing.

Not the ragged, inhuman gasps of the infected. This was slower, heavier.

She exchanged a glance with Elara, who nodded grimly. They

pushed the doors open just enough to slip inside, their eyes adjusting to the dim light.

What they saw made Kasai's blood run cold.

The gymnasium was filled with people. But they weren't moving.

Dozens of them, maybe more, sat in rows on the floor, their backs straight, their hands resting on their knees. Their eyes were open, but they stared straight ahead, unblinking. It was like they were in some kind of trance.

At the front of the room stood a man, his back to them. He was tall, wearing a ragged suit that hung loosely on his thin frame. His hands were clasped behind his back, and he was speaking in a low, rhythmic tone that Kasai couldn't quite make out.

But whatever he was saying, the people were *listening*.

Kasai's stomach twisted into knots. This wasn't a safe zone. This was something else.

Elara leaned in close, her voice barely a whisper. "We need to get out of here. *Now.*"

Kasai nodded, but before they could move, the man at the front of the room stopped speaking. Slowly, he turned around, his eyes scanning the gym until they landed on Kasai and Elara.

His smile was slow and cold, spreading across his face like a crack in glass.

"Well," he said, his voice carrying easily through the silent room. "Look what we have here."

Kasai's blood ran cold. The people in the room turned their heads in perfect unison, their empty, lifeless eyes locking onto her.

And then they *moved.*

Not like the infected—jerky and erratic. These people moved smoothly, silently, as they rose to their feet and started toward her.

Kasai's heart pounded in her chest as she grabbed Elara's arm. "Run!"

They bolted out of the gym, slamming the doors shut behind them. Kasai could hear the people on the other side, moving steadily, methodically, like they weren't in any hurry.

The others were waiting in the hallway, their eyes wide with fear as Kasai and Elara burst through the doors.

"What the hell is going on?" Riley hissed, her voice sharp with panic.

Kasai didn't have time to explain. She just grabbed Milo by the arm and shoved him toward the exit. "*Move!*"

They sprinted through the darkened hallways, the sounds of footsteps echoing behind them. Not frantic, but steady. Like whoever—or *whatever*—was following them knew they'd catch up eventually.

They burst out of the community center and into the night, their breath coming in ragged gasps. But the streets weren't empty anymore.

The infected were everywhere, drawn by the noise, their snarls echoing off the buildings.

Kasai's heart sank. They were surrounded.

But she wasn't going down without a fight.

She raised her wrench, her jaw set with grim determination.

They were still alive.

And as long as they were breathing, they had a chance.

62 hours left.

The infected closed in, their guttural snarls blending with the sound of shuffling feet and the steady, rhythmic footsteps of the people from the gym. It was a horrifying symphony—one that made Kasai's heart pound so loudly she could barely hear anything else.

The narrow street in front of the community center was a chaos of shadows and flickering light. Fires burned in the distance, casting eerie, dancing shapes against the buildings. The infected moved like predators, their milky eyes locking onto Kasai and the others, while the people from the gym advanced behind them, their expressions blank and their movements unsettlingly calm.

Kasai gripped her wrench tighter, feeling the cold metal bite into her palm. "We need to move. *Now.*"

Riley was already scanning the street, her sharp eyes searching for an escape route. "Alley to the left!" she shouted, pointing toward a narrow gap between two crumbling buildings.

Without hesitation, they sprinted toward the alley. The infected roared behind them, their footsteps turning into a frenzied stampede as they gave chase.

Kasai's lungs burned with every breath, but she didn't dare slow down. She could hear Milo's ragged breathing just behind her, followed by Caleb and his group—the two younger girls sobbing quietly as Sarah tried to keep them moving.

They darted into the alley, the walls closing in around them as they pushed deeper into the maze of backstreets. The narrow passageway twisted and turned, littered with debris and broken glass that crunched under their feet.

Kasai risked a glance over her shoulder and felt her stomach drop. The infected were gaining on them, their twisted faces illuminated by the flickering fires. But what unsettled her more were the people from the gym. They weren't running. They didn't *have* to. Their steady, relentless pace made it clear—they weren't going to stop until they found them.

"We need to find somewhere to hide!" Milo gasped, his voice high with panic.

"No hiding!" Elara barked, her tone sharp and commanding. "We keep moving. We stop, we die."

Kasai spotted an old fire escape ahead, its rusted metal ladder dangling just out of reach. "There!" she shouted, sprinting toward it.

Riley was the first to reach the ladder. She jumped, grabbing the bottom rung and pulling it down with a loud *clang* that echoed through the alley. "Up, now!" she hissed, waving them forward.

Kasai pushed Milo toward the ladder, giving him a boost as he scrambled up. Caleb helped Sarah and the girls next, their small hands trembling as they climbed.

Kasai was halfway up when she heard the infected slam into the base of the ladder, their claws scraping against the metal. She felt the whole structure shake beneath her, but she kept climbing, her heart pounding in her chest.

Riley reached the rooftop first, pulling Milo up behind her. Kasai scrambled over the edge a second later, grabbing Elara's hand as the older woman hauled her to safety. Caleb and his group followed, their faces pale and terrified.

They didn't stop to catch their breath. The infected were already trying to climb the fire escape, their snarls filling the night air.

Kasai led them across the rooftop, her eyes scanning for another escape route. The buildings were close together, their rooftops connected by precarious gaps and narrow ledges.

"We can jump to the next roof!" she shouted, pointing to a building a few feet away.

Riley didn't hesitate. She sprinted toward the edge and leaped, landing in a crouch on the other side. "Let's go!"

Milo followed, his legs trembling as he barely cleared the gap. Caleb helped the younger girls across, their small bodies light enough to toss safely to the other side.

Kasai took a deep breath and ran, her heart leaping into her throat as she sailed over the gap. She landed hard, her knees buckling, but she forced herself to keep moving.

Elara was the last to jump, her landing smooth and controlled. They didn't stop, weaving across the rooftops as the infected howled behind them, their screams echoing off the buildings.

By the time they reached the far end of the block, Kasai's legs felt like they were going to give out. She dropped to her knees, gasping for breath, her chest burning with exhaustion.

But they were alive. For now.

They found a moment of respite in an old apartment building, the rooftop access door miraculously unlocked. They slipped inside, bolting the door behind them as they collapsed in the darkened stairwell.

Kasai pressed her back against the cold wall, her heart still racing. She could hear the others breathing heavily around her, the weight of what they'd just survived settling over them like a heavy blanket.

Caleb held his daughters close, whispering soft reassurances as they clung to him, their small bodies trembling. Sarah sat against the wall, her face pale and her eyes distant, while Jason stared blankly at the floor, his knife still clutched tightly in his hand.

Milo let out a shaky breath, his voice barely audible. "What... what *were* those people?"

Kasai shook her head, her mind still struggling to process what they'd seen. "I don't know," she whispered. "But they weren't normal."

"They weren't infected," Elara added quietly, her eyes narrowing in thought. "But they weren't *right* either."

Riley let out a bitter laugh, her voice sharp in the silence. "Great. As if the infected weren't bad enough, now we've got creepy cult people to worry about."

Kasai closed her eyes, trying to steady her breathing. The world was falling apart faster than she could keep up with, and every time she thought they'd found some semblance of safety, it was ripped away.

But they couldn't afford to fall apart. Not now.

"We'll rest here for a bit," she said finally, forcing her voice to stay steady. "Then we'll figure out our next move."

The others nodded, their exhaustion too heavy for any arguments.

Kasai let her head fall back against the wall, her eyes drifting closed for just a moment. She could still hear the distant sounds of the infected outside, their snarls and screams a constant reminder that they were never truly safe.

But they were alive.

And as long as they were breathing, they had a chance.

61 hours left.

The stairwell was cloaked in suffocating silence, broken only by the distant snarls of the infected and the occasional creak of the old building settling. The walls were stained with grime, the peeling paint curling like dead leaves. The air was thick with dust, the faint smell of mold clinging to the back of Kasai's throat. But for the moment, it was shelter. A fragile barrier between them and the chaos outside.

Kasai sat with her back against the cold concrete wall, the weight of exhaustion pressing down on her like a heavy blanket. Her wrench rested in her lap, the metal cool against her skin, a small comfort in a world that had offered none. She closed her eyes for a brief second, letting the rhythm of her heartbeat slow, though the images flashing behind her eyelids kept any real rest at bay.

She could still see the faces of those people in the gym—their blank, unblinking eyes, the eerie synchronicity of their movements, and the man leading them, his voice a low, hypnotic drone. She didn't know what they were, but she knew one thing for certain. They were dangerous. Maybe even more dangerous than the infected.

Elara sat nearby, sharpening her makeshift blade with slow, deliberate movements. The rhythmic scrape of metal on metal was oddly soothing, a reminder that even in this chaos, there were still things within their control. Elara's calm presence had become an anchor for Kasai, a steady hand guiding them through the storm. But even now, Kasai could see the tension in her eyes, the tight set of her jaw.

Milo was curled up on the opposite side of the stairwell, his back pressed against the wall, his knees pulled to his chest. His baseball bat rested beside him, his fingers tapping anxiously against his leg. He hadn't said much since they escaped the community center, and Kasai could see the fear lingering in his eyes. The events of the day were taking their toll, and Kasai wondered how much longer they could all keep going.

Riley paced back and forth near the stairwell door, her movements sharp and restless. She kept glancing at the small, dirt-streaked window above the door, her jaw clenched tight. "We can't stay here all night," she muttered, more to herself than anyone else. "They'll find us. They *always* find us."

Kasai opened her eyes and let out a slow breath. "We're not moving until we're ready. We need to rest, even if it's just for a little while."

Riley shot her a sharp look. "And what if resting gets us killed? You saw what's out there, Kasai. Those people... they weren't normal."

Kasai nodded the weight of Riley's words settling in her chest. "I know. But running ourselves into the ground won't help, either. We need to be able to fight if we have to."

Riley didn't argue, but the tension in her shoulders didn't ease. She went back to pacing, her eyes flicking to the door every few seconds like she expected it to burst open at any moment.

Caleb and his group were huddled in the corner, their faces pale and drawn. Sarah held Emma and Lucy close, whispering soft reassurances into their hair, though her own eyes were filled with the same fear she was trying to keep from them. Jason sat apart from them, his knife resting on his knee, his gaze distant and unfocused.

Kasai watched them for a moment, her chest tightening with a mixture of guilt and responsibility. They hadn't asked for this. None of them had. But now they were part of this fragile, mismatched group, and Kasai felt the weight of their survival pressing down on her like a stone.

Elara's voice broke the heavy silence. "We need a plan."

Kasai nodded, forcing herself to focus. "The community center was a dead end. But there has to be somewhere else. Somewhere safe."

Caleb looked up, his expression grim. "There's no safe place out there. We've been running forever, and everywhere we go, it's the same. Infected, chaos, people turning on each other." He shook his head, his eyes darkening. "I don't think anyone's coming to help us."

Kasai clenched her jaw, refusing to let the hopelessness settle in. She thought of the emergency broadcast, the robotic voice that had echoed through the city: *"Help will arrive in 72 hours. Stay alive."*

It was the only thing keeping her moving.

"We don't know that," Kasai said, her voice firmer than she felt. "We have to believe that someone's out there. That help is coming."

Caleb didn't argue, but his eyes said he didn't believe her.

Elara leaned forward, her eyes sharp and focused. "There's an old train yard on the outskirts of the city. It's far from here, but if we can make it, the tunnels might offer us some cover. And if the military is coming, they'll use places like that for transport."

Riley snorted, crossing her arms over her chest. "That's a big *if*. But it's better than sitting here waiting to die."

Kasai nodded, her heart pounding in her chest. The train yard was a risk, but it was the best shot they had. "We'll move at first light. Rest while you can."

The others settled into uneasy silence, the exhaustion pulling them into restless sleep one by one. But Kasai couldn't close her eyes. She stared at the door, her fingers wrapped tightly around her wrench, listening to the distant sounds of the city unraveling.

The night stretched on, long and suffocating. Every creak of the building, every distant scream set her nerves on edge. She could feel the minutes slipping away, the hours ticking down like a countdown to something she couldn't see but knew was coming.

As dawn began to break, painting the sky in pale shades of pink and gray, Kasai finally let herself breathe. She stood, her muscles stiff and aching, and looked out the small window above the door.

The streets were quiet. Too quiet.

She turned back to the others, her voice low but steady. "It's time."

They moved through the building like shadows, slipping out the back entrance and into the cold morning air. The city was still, the usual sounds of chaos replaced by an eerie silence that made Kasai's skin crawl.

They stuck to the back alleys, avoiding the main roads, their footsteps light on the cracked pavement. The train yard was miles away, but Kasai kept her eyes forward, her mind focused on the goal ahead.

But as they moved deeper into the city, Kasai felt the familiar prick of anxiety crawling up her spine. The streets were too empty, the silence too complete. It was like the city was holding its breath, waiting for something.

They were halfway to the train yard when they saw it.

A barricade of abandoned cars and debris blocked the street ahead, and behind it, a group of people stood, their faces hidden behind makeshift masks and bandanas. They were armed—pipes, bats, and even a few guns glinting in the early morning light.

Kasai's heart sank. These weren't survivors looking for help. They were predators.

The leader stepped forward, a tall man with wild eyes and a cruel smile. "Looks like we've got some fresh meat," he drawled, his voice loud in the quiet street. "Hand over your supplies, and maybe we'll let you live."

Kasai tightened her grip on her wrench, her heart pounding in her chest. She could feel the others tense behind her, their fear palpable in the cold morning air.

But Kasai wasn't going down without a fight.

She met the man's gaze, her jaw set with grim determination. "You'll have to kill me first."

The man's smile widened. "Gladly."

And then all hell broke loose.

60 hours left.

Chapter 5
Blood and Betrayal

The street exploded into chaos.

Kasai barely had time to register the leader's twisted grin before his group surged forward, weapons raised and shouts piercing the morning air. The clash of metal against metal echoed through the empty streets, mingling with the distant, guttural growls of the infected that had undoubtedly been drawn by the noise.

Kasai lunged to the side as a rusted crowbar swung toward her head, the force of the near miss sending a sharp gust of air past her cheek. She felt the adrenaline surge through her veins like fire, burning away the exhaustion as she swung her wrench upward with all the strength she had. The solid *crack* of metal meeting bone reverberated through her arms as the attacker crumpled to the ground, clutching his bleeding head.

"*Move!*" Elara's voice cut through the noise, sharp and commanding. She was already in motion, her makeshift blade flashing as she deflected a swing from one of the raiders. With practiced precision, she slashed at the man's thigh, sending him sprawling with a howl of pain.

Riley was a blur of motion at Kasai's side, her knife glinting in the morning light as she ducked and weaved, her movements quick and vicious. She drove her blade into the gut of a man who had lunged at Milo, yanking it free with a grunt as he collapsed, gasping for breath.

Milo stood frozen for a moment, his wide eyes locked on the dying man at his feet. But then, as if a switch flipped, he let out a ragged scream and swung his baseball bat with wild desperation, catching another raider square in the jaw with a sickening *crunch.*

Kasai's heart pounded in her chest as she scanned the chaos. Caleb was shielding Emma and Lucy behind an overturned car, his face pale but determined as he swung a broken pipe at anyone who came too close. Sarah and Jason were nearby, the teenage boy's face twisted in fear as he slashed with his small knife, barely fending off an older, stronger raider.

Kasai's gaze snapped back to the leader—the man with the cruel smile. He stood at the center of it all, watching the fight unfold like it was a game. His eyes locked onto Kasai, and that twisted grin widened.

"You've got spirit, girl," he called over the noise, his voice dripping with mock admiration. "But spirit won't save you."

Kasai's grip tightened on her wrench. "We'll see about that."

The leader stepped forward, swinging a heavy metal chain in slow, deliberate circles. The links clinked together, an ominous sound that made Kasai's skin crawl.

Without another word, he lunged.

Kasai barely managed to dodge the first swing, the chain whistling through the air inches from her face. She countered with a wild swing of her own, aiming for his ribs, but he was fast—too fast. He sidestepped easily, the chain snapping out again, catching her shoulder and sending a jolt of pain down her arm.

She gritted her teeth, refusing to back down.

Out of the corner of her eye, she saw Elara struggling with two raiders at once, her movements slower than before, her face slick with sweat and blood. Riley was pinned against a wall by a hulking man twice her size, her knife struggling to find a gap in his defenses.

They were outnumbered. And they were losing.

Kasai ducked another swing, her mind racing. They couldn't win this fight head-on. They needed an advantage—something to tip the scales.

And then she heard it.

The distant, familiar shrieks of the infected.

Kasai's heart leaped into her throat. The noise had drawn them in. They didn't have much time.

"*Elara!*" she shouted, dodging another swipe from the leader's chain. "We need to move! The infected are coming!"

Elara's eyes snapped to hers, and in that instant, Kasai saw the same realization flash across her face.

"*Everyone, fall back!*" Elara barked, her voice cutting through the chaos like a blade.

Kasai swung her wrench one last time, catching the leader off guard and sending him stumbling back. She didn't wait to see if he recovered. She turned and ran, her heart pounding in her chest as she sprinted toward the others.

"*Go! Go!*" Riley shouted, finally breaking free from her attacker and grabbing Milo by the arm, dragging him toward the alley.

Caleb scooped up Emma and Lucy, their small bodies clinging to him as he ran, while Sarah and Jason followed close behind, their faces pale with terror.

They barreled down the alley, the sounds of the infected growing louder with every step. Kasai could hear the raiders shouting behind them, their cries turning to screams as the infected descended upon them.

Kasai didn't look back.

They emerged from the alley onto another street, their breath coming in ragged gasps. The city stretched out before them, a maze of crumbling buildings and flickering fires, but Kasai didn't care. All that mattered was getting as far away from the infected—and the raiders—as possible.

They ran until their legs gave out, finally collapsing in a

narrow, shadowed courtyard behind an old apartment building. The sounds of the infected were distant now, but Kasai knew they weren't safe. They were never safe.

She leaned back against the cold brick wall, her chest heaving as she tried to catch her breath. Her body ached, every muscle screaming in protest, but she was alive.

They all were.

For now.

Elara sank down beside her, her face pale but steady. "That was too close," she muttered, wiping blood from her forehead.

Kasai nodded, too exhausted to respond.

Milo sat on the ground a few feet away, his face buried in his hands. Riley hovered nearby, her knife still clutched tightly in her hand, her eyes darting to every shadow.

Caleb and his group were huddled together, the girls crying softly into his chest while Sarah whispered soothing words that sounded hollow even to Kasai's ears. Jason sat apart from them, his knife lying forgotten in his lap, his eyes staring blankly at the ground.

For a long time, no one spoke.

Finally, Kasai broke the silence. "We can't keep running like this."

Elara nodded, her eyes hardening. "We need a new plan."

Kasai looked out at the darkened city, her heart heavy but her resolve stronger than ever.

They had survived another day. But the clock was still ticking. And there were still **60 hours left**.

The cold pressed in around them as the sun dipped below the horizon, casting long shadows across the crumbling courtyard. Kasai pulled her knees to her chest, trying to ignore the dull ache in her muscles and the sting of fresh bruises blossoming along her ribs. The others sat in a loose circle, their faces pale and drawn, the weight of exhaustion settling over them like a thick fog. But it wasn't just the physical toll of the last few hours that weighed on them—it was the realization that the world outside was far worse than any of them had imagined.

Not only were the infected a constant threat, but now there were *people*—desperate, dangerous people—who were willing to kill for scraps, for control, or simply out of cruelty. And those strangers in the gym... Kasai shivered, remembering their blank stares and unnatural, synchronized movements. She didn't know what was happening to the world, but it felt like something deeper, something darker than just an outbreak.

Elara sat next to her, sharpening her blade with slow, deliberate strokes. The rhythmic sound of metal against stone was oddly comforting, a small piece of normalcy in the chaos. Elara's calm presence was a steady anchor for all of them, but Kasai could see the tension in her eyes, the tightness in her jaw. She was holding it together for their sake, but Kasai wondered how much longer they could all keep up the facade.

Riley leaned against the opposite wall, her arms crossed tightly over her chest. Her knife rested in her lap, but her eyes were sharp and alert, constantly scanning the shadows for any sign of movement. She hadn't said much since they escaped the raiders, but the anger simmering beneath her surface was palpable.

Milo sat hunched over beside her, his baseball bat resting across his knees. He was shaking slightly, his eyes fixed on the ground like he was trying to disappear into it. Every now and then, his lips would move silently, like he was replaying the events of the day over and over in his head, trying to make sense of it all.

Caleb's group was huddled in the corner, Emma and Lucy curled up against their father's chest, their small bodies trembling with exhaustion and fear. Sarah sat close by, her arm wrapped protectively around Jason's shoulders, though the boy seemed distant, his eyes glassy and unfocused.

The silence stretched on, heavy and oppressive. Finally, Elara broke it.

"We can't stay here," she said quietly, her voice steady but firm. "The infected will keep moving through the city, and those raiders might still be out there looking for us."

Kasai nodded, her heart sinking. She knew Elara was right. They couldn't afford to stay in one place for too long. But the thought of moving again, of facing whatever horrors waited for them in the dark streets, made her stomach twist with dread.

"There's the train yard," Riley said suddenly, her voice cutting through the silence like a blade. "It's still our best shot."

Kasai glanced at her, surprised by the certainty in her tone. Riley met her gaze, her eyes hard and determined.

"If the military's coming, that's where they'll set up," Riley continued. "And even if they're not, it's better cover than this."

Milo let out a shaky breath, his voice barely more than a whisper. "What if there's nothing there? What if it's just... more of *them*?"

Riley's jaw tightened. "Then we keep moving."

Kasai felt a flicker of admiration for Riley's resolve, even if it felt like they were clinging to hope by the thinnest of threads. But she knew they didn't have a choice. They had to believe there was something better out there.

She pushed herself to her feet, wincing as her bruised muscles protested. "We'll leave at first light," she said, glancing around the circle. "Rest while you can. We'll need the energy."

The others nodded, settling into uneasy silence once more. Kasai sat back down, but sleep felt like a distant dream. Her mind raced with thoughts of the gym, of the raiders, of the infected that seemed to multiply with every passing hour.

She thought of her mom, too—the last message she'd received before the world fell apart. *"Lock the doors. Don't let anyone in. I love you."* Kasai wondered if her mother was still out there somewhere, fighting to survive like they were. Or if she'd already fallen victim to the chaos.

The night stretched on, long and restless. Kasai drifted in and out of shallow sleep, her dreams filled with flashes of blood and fire, of blank, lifeless eyes, and the sound of chains clinking in the dark.

When the first light of dawn crept over the horizon, painting the sky in pale shades of pink and gray, Kasai was already awake. She stood, stretching her stiff limbs and scanning the courtyard for any signs of movement. The city was quiet, but Kasai knew better than to trust the silence.

"Time to go," Elara said softly, her voice pulling Kasai from her thoughts.

The others stirred, groaning and rubbing sleep from their eyes. Milo looked even paler than before, dark circles under his eyes, but he didn't complain as he grabbed his bat and followed the others.

They moved through the city like shadows, sticking to the alleys and side streets, avoiding the main roads where the infected were more likely to roam. The air was thick with tension, every sound amplified by the stillness of the morning.

As they neared the train yard, Kasai felt her heart begin to race. The sprawling complex of rusted tracks and abandoned cars loomed in the distance, surrounded by tall, chain-link fences topped with barbed wire. It looked deserted, but Kasai knew better than to assume anything.

They slipped through a gap in the fence, their footsteps muffled by the gravel beneath their feet. The train yard was eerily quiet, the only sounds were the distant calls of crows and the faint rustle of the wind through the abandoned cars.

Kasai scanned the area, her eyes darting from shadow to shadow, but there was no sign of movement. No infected. No people.

For a moment, it felt like they'd found a safe place.

But then Elara's hand shot out, grabbing Kasai's arm and pulling her down behind an old freight car. Kasai's heart leaped into her throat as she followed Elara's gaze.

At the far end of the train yard, a group of people moved between the cars, their movements quick and deliberate. They were armed, but they weren't raiders. They wore military gear, their weapons sleek and well-maintained.

Kasai felt a surge of hope rises in her chest. The military. *Help had arrived.*

But then she saw the prisoners.

A line of people, their hands bound behind their backs, being herded toward one of the larger train cars. Their faces were pale and hollow, their bodies thin and malnourished. And the soldiers—the ones who were supposed to protect them—were shoving them forward with the butts of their rifles, barking orders in harsh, clipped tones.

Kasai's stomach twisted. This wasn't a rescue.

Elara's grip on her arm tightened. "We need to get out of here. *Now.*"

But before they could move, one of the soldiers shouted, pointing directly at them.

"*There!*"

The courtyard erupted into chaos once more as the soldiers raised their weapons and advanced.

Kasai's heart pounded in her chest as she grabbed Milo's arm, pulling him to his feet.

"*Run!*" she screamed, her voice raw with panic.

And they did.

Through the maze of train cars, the sound of gunfire rang in their ears.

The world was falling apart.

And the people they thought would save them were the ones they now had to fear the most.

59 hours left.

Gunfire cracked through the air, sharp and unforgiving, ricocheting off the rusted metal of the train cars. Kasai's heart pounded in her chest as she sprinted through the maze of tracks, her breath coming in ragged gasps. The world blurred around her—shouts from the soldiers, the distant wails of the infected, and the thudding of her own footsteps on gravel merging into one chaotic symphony.

She gripped Milo's arm tightly, refusing to let him fall behind. His face was pale, drenched in sweat, but he kept moving, his legs churning through sheer adrenaline. Behind them, Elara and Riley darted between train cars, covering the group's retreat with sharp, precise movements. Caleb, Sarah, and the kids struggled to keep up, fear etched into every line of their faces.

This wasn't supposed to happen.

They'd risked everything to get here. The community center had been a trap, the raiders nearly killed them, and now the military—the *last* hope Kasai had clung to—wasn't here to rescue anyone. They were here to control, to dominate, to *enslave*.

The sound of boots pounding against the gravel behind them grew louder. The soldiers were closing in.

"This way!" Riley shouted, veering toward a narrow gap between two rusted boxcars. She slid through effortlessly, her small frame disappearing into the shadows. Kasai shoved Milo ahead of her, pushing him through the narrow space before following close behind.

They burst out into a small clearing, surrounded on all sides by towering stacks of abandoned shipping containers. The space was suffocating, the walls of rusted metal closing in on them like a cage.

"We can't outrun them!" Milo gasped, collapsing against a container, his chest heaving.

Kasai's mind raced, panic clawing at the edges of her thoughts. They couldn't run forever. They needed a plan.

Elara skidded to a stop beside them, her eyes sharp and calculating even as her breath came in short bursts. "We fight," she said simply, her voice calm despite the chaos.

Riley let out a bitter laugh, shaking her head. "Fight? Against *them*? They've got guns, Elara."

Kasai felt the weight of the situation presses down on her like a stone. Riley was right. The soldiers were armed, trained, and ruthless. But what other choice did they have?

She looked around the clearing, her eyes landing on a rusted ladder leading to the top of one of the containers. An idea sparked in her mind—risky, dangerous, but maybe their only shot.

"We split up," Kasai said, her voice steady despite the fear churning in her stomach. "Riley and I will draw them away. Elara, you take the others and find another way out."

Elara's eyes narrowed, but she didn't argue. She understood the stakes.

"You sure about this?" Riley asked, her voice low.

Kasai nodded, gripping her wrench tighter. "It's the only way."

Riley gave a sharp nod, the faintest hint of a smile tugging at the corner of her lips. "Alright, let's give them hell."

Kasai turned to Elara, her heart heavy. "We'll meet you at the old overpass on 5th. If we're not there by nightfall..." She let the words hang in the air.

Elara's jaw tightened, but she nodded. "You'll be there."

Kasai offered Milo a small, reassuring smile, even though her heart felt like it was breaking. "Stay close to Elara. You'll be okay."

Milo nodded, his eyes wide with fear but filled with trust. "You too."

Kasai didn't let herself linger. She turned and scrambled up the rusted ladder, Riley hot on her heels. They reached the top of the container and sprinted across the metal surface, the sound of gunfire growing louder behind them.

They reached the edge of the container stack and dropped down into another alley of train cars, landing hard on the gravel below. Kasai's knees screamed in protest, but she forced herself to her feet, adrenaline driving her forward.

Riley grabbed a loose piece of metal from the ground and hurled it against a nearby train car, the loud *clang* echoing through the yard.

"Over here, assholes!" she shouted, her voice ringing out across the tracks.

The soldiers' shouts grew louder, and Kasai could hear them changing direction, drawn by the noise. She and Riley sprinted down the alley, weaving between cars and containers, leading the soldiers deeper into the yard.

Kasai's lungs burned, her legs threatening to give out, but she didn't stop. She couldn't.

They reached the far end of the yard, where the train tracks disappeared into a dark tunnel. Kasai skidded to a stop, her heart pounding in her chest. The tunnel was a gamble—dark, dangerous, and likely filled with infected—but it was their only option.

Riley shot her a glance, her eyes gleaming with adrenaline. "After you."

Kasai took a deep breath and plunged into the darkness, the

sound of boots and gunfire fading behind them.

The tunnel was cold and damp, the air thick with the stench of mildew and decay. Their footsteps echoed off the walls, mingling with the distant, haunting moans of the infected.

Kasai's heart raced as they moved deeper into the tunnel, the darkness pressing in around them like a living thing. But she refused to let fear consume her. They'd made it this far. They would survive.

They had to.

After what felt like an eternity, they emerged from the tunnel into the dim light of an abandoned subway station. The space was eerily quiet, the flickering lights casting long, twisted shadows across the walls.

Kasai leaned against a pillar, her chest heaving as she tried to catch her breath. Riley collapsed beside her, a bitter laugh escaping her lips.

"Well," Riley panted, "that was fun."

Kasai let out a shaky laugh, the tension finally beginning to ease from her shoulders. But the relief was short-lived.

They still had to find Elara and the others.

They still had to survive the next **59 hours**.

The flickering lights of the abandoned subway station buzzed overhead, casting long, jittery shadows across the cracked tile floor. The cold seeped into Kasai's skin as she leaned against the rusted pillar, every muscle in her body aching from the sprint through the tunnel. Her chest heaved, trying to suck in air thick with dust and decay. She could still hear the echo of gunfire ringing in her ears, even though the soldiers' shouts had long faded into silence.

Riley sat beside her, back pressed against the same pillar, her knife resting loosely in her lap. She was breathing hard, but her eyes remained sharp, constantly scanning the shadows for movement. The adrenaline hadn't worn off yet—it was the only thing keeping them upright.

Kasai wiped the sweat from her brow with a trembling hand. "You think they got out?"

Riley didn't answer right away. She stared ahead, the flickering light reflecting off her eyes, making them seem even more hollow. Finally, she shrugged, her voice low and dry. "Elara's smart. They'll make it."

Kasai nodded, wanting to believe that. Elara was the strongest of them all—steady, calm, always thinking ahead. If anyone could get the others out, it was her. But Kasai couldn't shake the image of Milo's terrified face as they'd split up,or the sound of gunfire that had followed them as they ran.

For a moment, they sat in silence, the oppressive stillness of the station wrapping around them like a shroud. Then Kasai pushed herself to her feet, wincing as her legs protested.

"We can't stay here," she whispered.

Riley followed, gripping her knife tighter. "Yeah, no shit."

They moved cautiously through the station, their footsteps echoing off the grimy walls. The place was a tomb—abandoned long before the world had fallen apart. Dust-covered benches lined the platform, and old, faded advertisements hung crookedly from the walls, their bright colors dulled by years of neglect.

Kasai's eyes darted to every shadow, every darkened doorway. She could feel the tension coiling tighter with every step. They weren't safe. They *wouldn't* be safe until they found Elara and the others.

As they rounded a corner, they stumbled upon a broken vending machine, its glass shattered and contents long since picked clean. But wedged in the back, barely visible through the debris, was a single, unopened bottle of water.

Kasai's heart skipped. She rushed forward, yanking the bottle free and twisting off the cap. The water inside was warm and stale, but she didn't care. She handed it to Riley, who took a long gulp before passing it back.

Kasai drank deeply, feeling the cool liquid soothe her parched throat. It wasn't much, but it was something.

They continued deeper into the station, the faint sound of dripping water their only company. But then Kasai froze, her heart leaping into her throat.

Voices.

Distant, but unmistakable.

She grabbed Riley's arm, pulling her into the shadows of a nearby doorway. They crouched low, straining to listen. The voices grew louder, accompanied by the heavy clatter of boots on tile.

Soldiers.

Kasai's mind raced. *How had they found them so quickly?* She motioned for Riley to stay quiet, her heart pounding in her chest as the footsteps drew closer.

But as the group came into view, Kasai's breath caught in her throat.

It wasn't soldiers.

It was Elara.

Elara, Milo, Caleb, Sarah, Jason—and the girls.

Kasai felt a wave of relief wash over her so intensely that her legs nearly gave out. She stepped out of the shadows, her voice breaking with emotion.

"Elara!"

The group spun around, weapons raised, but the tension melted away the moment they saw Kasai and Riley.

Milo let out a strangled cry and rushed forward, throwing his arms around Kasai in a tight, desperate hug. She hugged him back, feeling tears sting her eyes.

"You made it," he whispered, his voice cracking.

Kasai pulled back just enough to look at him, her heart aching at the fear still lingering in his eyes. "So did you."

Elara approached, her face pale but otherwise calm. "We thought we lost you."

Kasai shook her head, wiping at her eyes. "We thought the same."

Riley clapped Milo on the back, her usual sharpness softened by relief. "Told you we'd meet up."

For a moment, they let themselves breathe, the weight of reunion dulling the ever-present fear. But it didn't last. It couldn't.

Elara's expression hardened. "We need to move. This place isn't safe."

Kasai nodded, the fleeting moment of relief already fading. "We saw soldiers in the train yard. They're... they're taking people. Not helping. *Enslaving* them."

Elara's jaw tightened. "I figured as much. We saw what they did to anyone who resisted." Her voice dropped, laced with anger. "They're not here to save anyone."

Kasai felt the last remnants of hope crumble in her chest. The broadcast had promised rescue. They'd clung to that promise and pushed themselves to the brink for it. But now it was clear—they were on their own.

"Where do we go?" Milo asked, his voice small.

Elara's eyes scanned the group, lingering on each face. "We head east. Get out of the city. The farther we are from the military and the infected, the better our chances."

Kasai swallowed hard. Leaving the city meant abandoning any last hope of finding her mom. But staying meant death—or worse. She had to believe her mom had found safety somewhere. She *had* to.

"Alright," Kasai whispered. "Let's go."

They moved as one, slipping back into the shadows of the subway tunnels. The air grew colder as they descended deeper into the underground, the weight of the city above pressing down on them.

Hours passed in a blur of darkness and quiet footsteps. The tension never eased, every shadow a potential threat, every distant sound a reminder of how fragile their survival was.

Eventually, they found an old maintenance tunnel that led to the surface. Elara motioned for silence as they climbed the rusted ladder, emerging into the pale light of dawn.

The city stretched out before them, a landscape of ruins and smoke. But beyond the crumbling skyline, Kasai saw something she hadn't seen in days.

The horizon.

Open, vast—and free.

They moved quickly, leaving the city behind as the sun rose higher in the sky. The road ahead was uncertain, filled with dangers they couldn't yet imagine. But for the first time in what felt like forever, Kasai felt a flicker of something she thought she'd lost.

Hope.

They were still alive.

And as long as they were breathing, they had a chance.

58 hours left.

The road out of the city felt endless.

The group trudged through the broken streets, the crumbling remains of civilization towering around them like skeletal giants. The sun was a faint smudge behind a layer of gray clouds, casting everything in a dull, lifeless light. The air was thick with the smell of smoke and decay, and every breath tasted like ash.

Kasai kept her eyes on the horizon, focusing on the faint, distant line where the city ended and the unknown began. Her body ached with every step, her legs heavy from exhaustion, but she didn't stop. None of them did. They couldn't afford to.

Riley walked beside her, silent but steady, her knife clenched tightly in one hand. Milo was just behind them, his baseball bat resting against his shoulder, though his grip had loosened with fatigue. Caleb and his daughters followed closely, the two young girls clinging to their father's hands, their faces pale and hollow. Sarah and Jason brought up the rear, their eyes darting nervously to every shadow.

Elara led the group, her posture rigid, her eyes scanning the ruined landscape for threats. She moved with the same calm, measured confidence she always did, but Kasai could see the tension in her shoulders, the way her fingers twitched near the hilt of her blade.

They'd been walking for hours, the silence between them growing heavier with each step. The events of the last day hung over them like a dark cloud—the betrayal at the community center, the ambush by the raiders, the soldiers in the train yard. It was too much to process, too much to carry. But they didn't have the luxury of falling apart. Not yet.

As they passed an overturned bus, its windows shattered and streaked with dried blood, Kasai felt a sharp pang of grief. She remembered riding buses like this with her mom, complaining about school, and laughing at stupid jokes. That world felt like a lifetime ago, a distant memory from someone else's life.

She wondered if her mom was still out there somewhere, hiding in the shadows, fighting to survive. Or if she'd already become another victim of the chaos.

Kasai shoved the thought down, focusing on the road ahead. She couldn't afford to dwell on what she couldn't control. All she could do was keep moving.

After what felt like an eternity, Elara finally slowed, raising a hand to signal the group to stop. They gathered around her, their breaths coming in ragged gasps.

"There's a small gas station up ahead," Elara said quietly, her eyes flicking to each of them. "We'll rest there for a bit, check for supplies."

Kasai nodded, her heart pounding in her chest. The thought of resting—even for a moment—felt like a small victory. But she knew better than to let her guard down.

They moved cautiously toward the gas station, sticking to the shadows and keeping their footsteps light. The building was small, its windows shattered, the front door hanging crookedly from its hinges. A rusted sign swung in the breeze, the faded letters barely legible beneath layers of grime.

They slipped inside, the air thick with the smell of gasoline and mildew. Kasai's eyes adjusted quickly to the dim light, scanning the aisles for any sign of movement. But the place was empty, just another ghost of the world that once was.

Elara motioned for them to spread out, to search for anything useful. Kasai moved down one of the aisles, her eyes scanning the shelves for food or water. Most of the shelves were bare, picked clean by looters long before they arrived. But tucked behind a stack of dusty cans, she found a single, unopened bottle of water and a granola bar.

She held the items in her hands, feeling the weight of them like they were treasures. She knew it wasn't enough—not for all of them—but it was something.

Riley appeared at her side, holding a small box of matches and a half-empty lighter. "Better than nothing," she muttered, stuffing the items into her bag.

Kasai nodded, slipping the water and granola bar into her own bag. They moved back toward the front of the store, where the others were gathered near the counter. Caleb sat on the floor with Emma and Lucy, their small bodies curled against his side. Milo leaned against the wall, his eyes distant, while Sarah and Jason whispered quietly in the corner.

Elara stood near the window, her eyes scanning the horizon. She didn't look up as Kasai and Riley approached, but her voice was low and steady. "We'll rest here for an hour, then we move."

Kasai dropped onto the floor beside Milo, feeling the exhaustion settle into her bones. She let her head fall back against the wall, closing her eyes for just a moment. The silence stretched on, heavy and suffocating, but it was a relief after everything they'd been through.

But the quiet didn't last.

A sound echoed through the stillness—a soft, rhythmic thumping, like footsteps on gravel.

Kasai's eyes snapped open, her heart leaping into her throat. She met Elara's gaze, seeing the same fear reflected in her eyes.

Someone was coming.

Elara moved quickly, her voice a sharp whisper. "Everyone, get down. Stay quiet."

They scrambled to hide, slipping behind shelves and counters, their breaths coming in shallow gasps. Kasai crouched behind the counter with Milo, her heart pounding in her chest. She gripped her wrench tightly, her knuckles white.

The footsteps grew louder, and closer until they were just outside the door.

Kasai held her breath, her entire body tense, waiting for the inevitable.

The door creaked open, the sound echoing through the small space.

Kasai risked a glance over the counter and felt her stomach drop.

It was a soldier.

But he was alone, his uniform torn and bloodstained, his face pale and gaunt. He moved slowly, his eyes darting around the room like a hunted animal.

Kasai's mind raced. *Was he dangerous? Was he one of the soldiers from the train yard?*

Elara stepped out from behind the shelves, her blade drawn but held low. "Who are you?" she demanded, her voice steady.

The soldier froze, his eyes widening in shock. He raised his hands slowly, his voice trembling. "I'm not here to hurt you. I— I escaped."

Kasai's heart pounded in her chest. *Escaped?*

Elara's eyes narrowed. "From where?"

The soldier swallowed hard, his gaze flicking to each of them. "The train yard. The others... they're not what you think. They're not here to help anyone. They're taking people— experimenting on them."

A cold chill ran down Kasai's spine. She thought of the people in the gym, their blank stares, their synchronized movements.

Elara's voice was low, dangerous. "What kind of experiments?"

The soldier's face twisted in fear. "I don't know. I heard things—screams, strange noises. They're trying to control the infected, make them... *obedient.* But it's not working. It's making them worse."

Kasai felt bile rise in her throat. The infected were already unstoppable. The idea of someone trying to control them—*use them*—was horrifying.

Elara lowered her blade slightly, but her eyes remained hard. "Why should we trust you?"

The soldier's shoulders sagged, and he let out a ragged breath. "You shouldn't. But I know a way out of the city. A safe route. If you let me help, I can get you there."

Kasai exchanged a glance with Elara. It was a risk—a big one. But they were running out of options.

Finally, Elara nodded. "You lead the way. But if you try anything..." She didn't finish the sentence, but the threat hung in the air like a blade.

The soldier nodded quickly, his eyes wide with fear. "I won't."

Kasai felt her heart pounding in her chest as they gathered their things. They were placing their trust in a stranger, but what other choice did they have?

They moved out of the gas station and back into the broken world, the soldier leading the way.

Kasai didn't know what lay ahead. But she knew one thing for sure.

They were still alive.

And as long as they were breathing, they had a chance.

57 hours left.

Chapter 6
The Path of Shadows

The soldier led them through the twisted remains of the city with a quiet, practiced efficiency, his boots crunching softly against the rubble-strewn streets. The rising sun cast long shadows across the broken landscape, painting the cracked asphalt and skeletal buildings in hues of orange and red. It should have been beautiful, but to Kasai, it looked like the world was bleeding.

She kept close to Elara, her grip tight around her wrench, every nerve on edge. The soldier—who had finally introduced himself as Daniel—walked ahead, his rifle slung low but his posture tense, like he expected an attack at any moment. Kasai didn't trust him. Not yet. Maybe not ever. But they were out of options, and if Daniel really knew a way out of the city, it was a risk they had to take.

Riley trailed just behind them, her knife glinting faintly in the morning light, while Milo hovered near Kasai, his eyes darting nervously to every shadow. Caleb and his daughters stayed in the middle of the group, Sarah and Jason bringing up the rear, their weapons clutched tightly in trembling hands. The girls were eerily quiet, their small faces pale and expressionless, like the fear had hollowed them out.

They moved in silence, the weight of exhaustion pressing down on them like a suffocating blanket. Every sound—the distant shriek of an infected, the clatter of debris kicked aside—made Kasai's heart leap into her throat. The city felt like a predator, watching them from the shadows, waiting for them to slip.

Daniel led them through a narrow alley between two crumbling apartment buildings, the walls covered in peeling paint and streaks of dried blood. The smell of decay was stronger here, clinging to the air like a toxic fog. Kasai fought the urge to gag, breathing through her mouth as they pressed on.

"We're close," Daniel murmured, his voice barely audible. "There's an old maintenance tunnel just ahead. It leads out of the city, under the perimeter fences. It's the only safe way I know."

Elara's eyes narrowed. "And why should we believe you?"

Daniel hesitated, his jaw tightening. "Because I was stationed there before everything went to hell. I saw what they were doing—the experiments, the camps. I barely got out alive."

Kasai didn't miss the tremor in his voice, the haunted look that flickered in his eyes. She wanted to believe him, but trust was a luxury she couldn't afford. Still, they followed him deeper into the alley, their footsteps echoing off the walls like ghosts.

As they rounded a corner, Kasai's stomach clenched. The alley opened up into a small courtyard, and at the far end, a metal door hung ajar, leading into the darkness of the maintenance tunnels. But something felt wrong. The hair on the back of her neck stood on end, and she could see Elara tense beside her.

"Wait," Elara whispered, grabbing Daniel's arm and pulling him to a stop. "Something's not right."

Daniel frowned, but before he could respond, a sharp click echoed through the courtyard.

Kasai's heart dropped.

They'd walked into a trap.

Figures emerged from the shadows, their faces obscured by makeshift masks and hoods. Armed with pipes, knives, and stolen rifles, they surrounded the group with predatory smiles, their eyes gleaming with malicious intent.

"Drop your weapons," a voice growled from behind one of the masked figures. The speaker stepped forward, revealing a gaunt, scarred face twisted into a cruel grin. "And maybe we'll let you live."

Kasai felt a surge of fury rises in her chest. They'd survived the infected, the soldiers, and now this? She tightened her grip on her wrench, refusing to back down.

Elara stepped forward, her blade glinting in the morning light. "We're not giving you anything."

The man chuckled, a cold, humorless sound. "Wrong answer."

Before Kasai could react, the man lunged, swinging a rusted machete toward Elara. But Elara was faster. She sidestepped the attack with practiced ease, driving her blade into his side with brutal precision. The man let out a strangled cry, collapsing to the ground as blood pooled beneath him.

Chaos erupted.

The masked attackers surged forward, and Kasai found herself in the middle of a violent, frenzied brawl. She swung her wrench with all her strength, the metal connecting with a sickening crack as it collided with the skull of one of the raiders. The man crumpled to the ground, but there were more—too many.

Riley fought like a demon beside her, her knife flashing as she slashed at anything that came too close. Milo screamed as he swung his bat wildly, his face twisted in terror. Kasai could hear Caleb shouting, trying to protect his daughters, while Sarah and Jason struggled to fend off their attackers.

Daniel was nowhere to be seen.

Kasai's heart pounded in her chest as she ducked a swing from another raider, driving her wrench into his knee and sending him sprawling. She didn't have time to think, didn't have time to process. It was just instinct now—survive.

But then she saw him.

Daniel.

He was standing at the edge of the courtyard, his rifle raised— not at the raiders, but at them. His face was calm, almost blank, as he took aim.

Kasai's blood ran cold.

"Betrayer!" Riley screamed, her voice hoarse with rage.

But before Daniel could pull the trigger, a sharp whistle cut through the air.

The raiders froze, their eyes snapping to Daniel, who lowered his rifle with a small, satisfied smile.

Kasai's heart sank as the truth hit her like a punch to the gut.

Daniel hadn't escaped the soldiers. He was working with them.

The leader of the raiders stepped forward, his face twisted into a cruel grin. "Good work, soldier."

Daniel nodded, his expression unreadable. "I told you they'd be easy to lead here."

Kasai's mind raced. How could we have been so stupid? She clenched her jaw, her heart pounding in her chest as the raiders surrounded them, their weapons raised.

But Elara wasn't done.

With a fierce cry, she lunged at Daniel, her blade flashing in the morning light. But Daniel was faster. He swung his rifle like a club, catching Elara in the side and sending her sprawling to the ground.

Kasai's rage boiled over.

With a roar, she charged at Daniel, her wrench raised high. But before she could reach him, a sharp pain exploded in her side, and she crumpled to the ground, gasping for breath.

The world spun around her, the sounds of the fight fading into a dull roar.

Through the haze of pain, she saw Daniel standing over her, his rifle pointed at her chest.

"This is the end," he said quietly, his voice devoid of emotion.

But Kasai wasn't ready to die.

With the last of her strength, she swung her wrench, catching Daniel in the knee. He stumbled, letting out a curse, but before he could recover, a gunshot echoed through the courtyard.

Daniel's eyes widened in shock, a dark stain blooming across his chest as he crumpled to the ground.

Kasai blinked, trying to focus through the pain.

Standing over Daniel's body was Milo, his hands shaking as he lowered the rifle he'd picked up from one of the fallen raiders.

The courtyard fell silent.

The raiders fled, their leader shouting orders as they disappeared into the shadows, leaving the group battered and bloodied but alive.

Kasai felt herself being lifted, strong arms wrapping around her as Elara's face came into view, her eyes filled with worry and determination.

"We're not done yet," Elara whispered. "You're going to make it."

Kasai nodded weakly, her vision fading.

They had survived.

But the fight wasn't over.

Not yet.

56 hours left.

Pain was Kasai's first companion as she drifted in and out of consciousness. It radiated from her side in hot, pulsing waves, each throbs a reminder that she was still alive. The world around her was a blur of sound and shadow—the distant echo of footsteps on gravel, hushed voices that seemed too far away, and the rhythmic pounding of her own heartbeat in her ears.

When her eyes finally fluttered open, the world came into hazy focus. She was lying on a dusty floor, the rough texture of cracked tiles pressing against her cheek. Faint light filtered through broken windows above, casting jagged beams across the room. She tried to move, but a sharp jolt of pain shot through her side, forcing a gasp from her lips.

"Easy."

Elara's voice was soft but firm, and Kasai felt a steady hand on her shoulder, grounding her. She turned her head slightly, wincing as her vision cleared enough to see Elara kneeling beside her, a ragged strip of cloth tied tightly around Kasai's torso, just beneath her ribs. The fabric was stained with blood—her blood.

"What... happened?" Kasai croaked, her voice barely a whisper.

Elara's eyes were tired but resolute. "You took a hit from one of the raiders. It's not deep, but you lost a lot of blood. We managed to stop the bleeding, but you're going to be sore for a while."

Kasai let out a shaky breath, her mind struggling to piece together the fractured memories. The ambush, Daniel's betrayal, the fight in the courtyard... and Milo. She blinked, her heart lurching in her chest.

"Milo," she whispered, trying to sit up.

Elara gently pressed her back down. "He's okay. We all are." She glanced over her shoulder. "Milo's the one who saved you. He shot Daniel."

Kasai's heart swelled with a mix of pride and guilt. She remembered the look on Milo's face as he pulled the trigger, the shock and horror of what he'd done. She wanted to find him, to tell him how brave he'd been, but the pain was too much.

"Where... are we?" she asked instead, her voice hoarse.

Elara glanced around the dimly lit room. "An old school. We found it after the raiders fled. It's not much, but it's shelter."

Kasai's eyes drifted around the space. The room was large, probably a classroom once, with faded posters peeling from the walls and rows of rusted desks pushed against the far side. The windows were cracked and dirty, but they offered enough light to see the others huddled together in the corner. Riley was sharpening her knife with slow, deliberate movements, while Milo sat nearby, his eyes fixed on the floor. Caleb held his daughters close, whispering softly to them, and Sarah and Jason sat quietly, their faces pale and drawn.

The weight of everything that had happened settled over Kasai like a heavy blanket. The world felt smaller now, darker. Daniel's betrayal had shattered what little trust she'd had left in humanity. They couldn't rely on anyone but themselves.

Elara's voice pulled her from her thoughts. "We need to move soon. The raiders might come back, and we're too exposed here."

Kasai nodded weakly, though the thought of moving made her stomach twist. She wasn't ready, but she knew Elara was right. They couldn't stay in one place for long.

Elara helped her sit up slowly, the pain sharp but bearable. Kasai gritted her teeth, focusing on the steady rhythm of her breathing. She couldn't afford to fall apart now. Not when they still had a chance.

Milo looked up as they approached, his eyes widening with relief when he saw Kasai awake. He scrambled to his feet, his hands trembling as he reached for her.

"Kasai!" he whispered, his voice thick with emotion. "I—I thought..."

Kasai managed a small, reassuring smile, though it felt like a lie. "I'm okay," she said softly, reaching out to squeeze his hand. "You saved me, Milo. You were... brave."

Milo's eyes filled with tears, and he shook his head. "I didn't want to... I didn't mean to..."

Kasai pulled him into a gentle hug, ignoring the sharp pain in her side. "You did what you had to do," she whispered. "You saved my life."

They stayed like that for a moment, the weight of everything they'd been through pressing down on them. But there was no time to dwell on the past. They had to keep moving.

Elara clapped her hands softly, drawing everyone's attention. "We need to head out," she said quietly, her eyes scanning the room. "There's a road that leads out of the city to the east. It's risky, but it's our best shot."

Riley stood, sliding her knife into her belt. "Let's get it over with."

Kasai forced herself to her feet, leaning on Milo for support. Every step sent a jolt of pain through her side, but she gritted her teeth and pushed forward. She wouldn't slow them down. She couldn't.

They moved through the abandoned school in silence, their footsteps echoing off the cracked linoleum floors. The hallways were littered with debris—old textbooks, broken lockers, faded photos of a world that no longer existed. Kasai's heart ached as she passed a bulletin board covered in cheerful drawings and notes from students who had probably never made it out.

The front doors creaked as they pushed them open, the bright sunlight blinding the dim interior. The city stretched outbefore them, a wasteland of broken buildings and burned-out cars. The road ahead was long and uncertain, but it was the only path left.

Elara led the way, her posture rigid and determined. Kasai followed closely, her eyes scanning the horizon for any sign of danger. The others moved in a tight formation, their faces grim but resolute.

As they walked, Kasai couldn't shake the feeling that they were being watched. The city felt alive like it was breathing, waiting for the right moment to strike. She kept her wrench tight in her hand, her heart pounding in her chest.

They passed through a narrow street lined with abandoned cars, their rusted frames casting long shadows across the pavement. Kasai's stomach twisted as she spotted a small, stuffed bear lying in the gutter, its fur matted and stained.

Suddenly, Elara held up a hand, signaling them to stop. Kasai's heart leaped into her throat as she followed Elara's gaze.

Up ahead, a group of infected stumbled into the street, their bodies twisted and broken, their eyes glowing with unnatural hunger.

Kasai's breath caught in her chest. They couldn't fight them— not in her condition, not with the kids.

Elara's voice was a low whisper. "We go around. Stay quiet. Stay low."

They moved quickly and silently, slipping between the shadows of the buildings. The infected didn't notice them, theirattention was focused elsewhere. But Kasai's heart didn't slow until they were several blocks away, the danger finally behind them.

They found shelter in an old convenience store, its windows boarded up, the interior dark and musty. Elara motioned for them to rest, and Kasai sank to the floor, her body screaming in protest.

Milo sat beside her, his eyes still wide with fear. "Do you think... do you think we'll make it?" he whispered.

Kasai looked at him, her heart aching for the boy who had lost so much in such a short time. She didn't have an answer. She didn't know what the next few hours would bring, let alone the next two days. But she knew one thing for sure.

"As long as we keep moving," she whispered, "we have a chance."

The group settled into a tense, uneasy silence, the weight of the world pressing down on them. But Kasai held onto that small flicker of hope, refusing to let it die.

They were still alive.

And as long as they were breathing, they had a chance.

55 hours left.

The stale air of the convenience store wrapped around Kasai like a suffocating blanket. Dust floated in the slanted beams of light slipping through the gaps in the boarded windows, and the faint stench of mildew clung to the cracked tiles beneath them. Kasai sat against a rusted metal shelf near the back of the store, her side throbbing with every shallow breath. The ragged strip of cloth Elara had tied around her torso felt damp and sticky, but the bleeding had slowed.

For now.

Milo sat close by, his knees drawn to his chest, his fingers absently picking at the frayed hem of his shirt. His wide eyes flicked between the boarded windows and Kasai's face as if needing constant reassurance that she was still there, still breathing. Kasai forced a weak smile whenever their eyes met, though the weight of exhaustion made it hard to keep up the pretense.

Elara crouched by the front door, her blade resting across her knees as she kept watch. Riley was near the windows, peeking through a sliver of light, her posture tense and ready. Caleb had found an old blanket in the corner and wrapped Emma and Lucy in it, holding them close as they drifted into a restless sleep. Sarah and Jason sat nearby, their expressions blank, their eyes hollowed out by fear and fatigue.

The silence was thick, pressing down on them like the weight of the city itself. Kasai hated it. Silence meant the world was waiting to throw something else at them. And in this new world, it was never a matter of if—only when.

After what felt like an eternity, Elara broke the silence. Her voice was soft, but it carried through the small space like a warning.

"They're still out there."

Kasai's heart skipped. "The raiders?"

Elara nodded, her eyes never leaving the crack in the door. "I saw movement a few blocks back. Could've been them... or worse."

Riley let out a soft curse under her breath, her fingers tightening around the hilt of her knife. "We can't sit here forever."

Kasai shifted, wincing as a fresh wave of pain shot through her side. "We don't have much of a choice. If they're out there, moving now could get us killed."

Riley turned toward her, eyes flashing. "And staying here will? What do you think happens when night falls, Kasai? We'll be sitting ducks in here."

Kasai opened her mouth to respond, but Elara's voice cut through the brewing tension. "We'll move at dusk."

The finality in her tone silenced any further argument. They trusted Elara—Kasai did, too. She was the closest thing they had to a leader, and in a world that had lost all sense of direction, that meant something.

The hours dragged on, each minute stretching into an eternity. The fading light outside marked the slow passage of time, turning the dusty store into a dim, oppressive cave. The group moved as little as possible, conserving their strength, their voices reduced to murmured whispers or silent glances.

Kasai's mind drifted in and out of focus, her thoughts tugged between the throbbing pain in her side and the gnawing worry for her mom. She pulled her phone from her pocket, even though she knew there wouldn't be any messages. The screen was cracked, the battery nearly dead, but she stared at the last text her mom had sent: "Lock the doors. Don't let anyone in. I love you."

Kasai swallowed hard, shoving the phone back into her pocket. She couldn't afford to think about it now. She needed to stay present—for Milo, for the others. But the ache in her chest was worse than the wound at her side.

As the sun dipped below the horizon, casting the city in hues of purple and gray, Elara finally stood.

"It's time."

The group stirred, groaning softly as they pushed themselves to their feet. Kasai gritted her teeth against the pain, leaning on Milo as she stood. She felt weak, but she wouldn't let it show. Not now.

Elara outlined their plan in hushed tones. "We stick to the alleys, avoid the main roads. The raiders won't expect us to move at night, but the infected will be more active. We move fast and stay quiet. No lights."

Kasai nodded, feeling the tension coil tighter in her chest. The infected were always worse at night—faster, more aggressive, as the darkness gave them strength. But staying in the store wasn't an option. They had to move.

The group slipped out of the convenience store like shadows, the cool night air biting at their skin. The city felt different in the dark, more alive in the worst possible way. Every sound—every distant scream or shuffle of feet—echoed off the buildings, amplifying their fear.

They moved in silence, their footsteps muffled against the cracked pavement. Kasai kept her eyes on Elara's back, focusing on the steady rhythm of her movements to keep herself grounded. Milo stayed close at her side, his small hand gripping her arm tightly.

As they weaved through narrow alleys and crumbling streets, Kasai's heart pounded in her chest. The city felt like a labyrinth, every turn revealing new dangers. Twice they had to duck behind cars or into dark doorways as groups of infected stumbled by, their grotesque forms illuminated by the flickering light of distant fires.

They'd just crossed an old intersection when Kasai felt it—a strange, low hum beneath her feet, like the city itself was vibrating. She froze, her breath catching in her throat.

"Elara..." she whispered, her voice barely audible.

Elara stopped, her head tilting slightly as she listened. The hum grew louder, a deep, mechanical rumble that seemed to be coming from somewhere up ahead.

Then, they saw it.

A convoy of military trucks rumbled down the main road, their headlights cutting through the darkness like knives. But these weren't rescue vehicles. The trucks were armored, their sides painted with hastily scrawled symbols, and in the back of one, Kasai saw a group of people—survivors—huddled together in chains.

Her blood ran cold.

The soldiers weren't just enslaving people. They were transporting them—moving them somewhere.

Kasai felt a surge of anger rises in her chest, burning away the fear. This wasn't just about survival anymore. It was about fighting back.

Elara pulled them back into the shadows, her face grim. "We keep moving. But we follow them."

Riley's eyes widened. "Are you insane? We can't take on a convoy."

Elara shook her head. "We're not attacking them. Not yet. But if they're moving people, we need to know where. There could be more survivors. Maybe even Kasai's mom."

The words hit Kasai like a punch to the gut. She hadn't dared to hope, not really. But now, the possibility sparked something inside her—a flicker of determination that refused to be extinguished.

They followed the convoy from a distance, sticking to the shadows, their hearts pounding with every turn. The trucks led them deeper into the city, toward an industrial district Kasai didn't recognize. The buildings here were larger, looming like silent sentinels in the dark, their windows shattered and walls scarred by fire.

The convoy finally stopped at a large warehouse, its exterior surrounded by barbed wire and makeshift barricades. Soldiers patrolled the perimeter, their rifles gleaming in the moonlight.

Kasai crouched behind a rusted dumpster, her breath coming in short gasps. Her side ached, but she ignored it, her focus locked on the warehouse. She could see the prisoners being herded inside, their faces pale and hollow.

Elara's voice was a low whisper in her ear. "We'll find a way in."

Kasai nodded, her heart pounding in her chest. They weren't just surviving anymore.

They were going to fight back.

54 hours left.

Kasai crouched behind the rusted dumpster, her heart slamming against her ribs like a warning drum. The warehouse loomed ahead, a monolithic structure of corrugated metal and crumbling concrete, its edges bathed in the cold, silver light of the moon. The barbed wire fencing around the perimeter glinted like jagged teeth, and armed guards patrolled in slow, deliberate circuits, their rifles cradled against their chests.

From their hiding spot, Kasai could see the prisoners being shuffled inside, their heads down, shoulders slumped. Chains clinked softly in the night air, an eerie counterpoint to the faint hum of generators somewhere deep within the compound. Every now and then, a muffled cry would escape from the warehouse's shadowed maw, followed by the sharp crack of a gun or the sickening thud of a body hitting concrete.

Kasai's stomach twisted, her breath catching in her throat. What are they doing to them?

Elara's hand settled on Kasai's shoulder, grounding her. "We don't have much time," she whispered, her voice steady despite the tension radiating from her. "We need to figure out how to get inside."

Kasai nodded, swallowing hard against the lump in her throat. Her mind raced, trying to piece together a plan, but the exhaustion and pain from her wound made it hard to think clearly. She glanced at the others—Riley, crouched low with her knife glinting faintly in the moonlight, her eyes hard and focused; Milo, his face pale but determined, gripping his baseball bat tightly; Caleb, holding Emma and Lucy close, whispering soft reassurances to them even as his own fear flickered in his eyes. Sarah and Jason stayed near the back, their expressions tense but ready.

Riley broke the silence first. "We can't just waltz in there," she muttered, her gaze flicking to the guards. "They'll mow us down before we even get close."

Elara nodded, her eyes scanning the perimeter. "We need a distraction."

Kasai's heart pounded harder. A distraction meant risk— someone would have to draw the guards away, and with the soldiers' ruthlessness, it wouldn't take much for things to spiral out of control.

"What about the generators?" Milo's voice was quiet but sure, surprising Kasai. He pointed toward a small building at the back of the warehouse, where the low hum of machinery was loudest. "If we can knock out the power, it might give us the edge we need."

Kasai's eyes widened slightly. That's... not a bad idea. In the dark, chaos would be their ally.

Elara's lips pressed into a thin line as she considered it. "It's risky," she murmured. "But it might be our only shot."

"I'll do it." Kasai's voice came out stronger than she felt, the words slipping out before she could think twice.

Elara's eyes snapped to hers, sharp and assessing. "You're still injured."

Kasai met her gaze, refusing to back down. "I can handle it."

Riley let out a soft scoff. "You've got more guts than sense."

"Maybe," Kasai shot back, "but guts are what's kept us alive this long."

Elara sighed, but there was a flicker of pride in her eyes. "Alright. But you're not going alone."

Riley straightened, her knife sliding back into her belt. "I'll go with her."

Kasai felt a surge of gratitude, though she didn't say it out loud. She knew Riley wasn't one for emotional speeches, and besides, they didn't have time for that now.

Elara turned to Milo. "Stay with Caleb and the others. Keep them safe. We'll signal when the power's out."

Milo nodded, his jaw tight with determination. Kasai reached out and squeezed his hand briefly before slipping away into the shadows with Riley.

The night pressed in around them as they crept along the fence line, their movements slow and deliberate. Every crunch of gravel beneath their feet sounded deafening, and Kasai's heart hammered in her chest with each step. Her side throbbed with a dull, persistent ache, but she forced herself to focus on the task ahead.

They reached the back of the compound without incident, the small utility building looming ahead. A single guard stood at the door, his rifle slung lazily over his shoulder, his posture relaxed but alert.

Riley leaned in close, her breath warm against Kasai's ear. "I'll take him out. Be ready to move."

Kasai nodded, her grip tightening on her wrench as Riley slipped into the shadows. She watched as Riley crept up behind the guard, her movements silent and fluid. With a swift, practiced motion, Riley's knife flashed in the moonlight, and the guard crumpled to the ground without a sound.

Kasai hurried forward, her heart pounding with adrenaline. Riley dragged the guard's body into the shadows before they slipped inside the utility building.

The interior was cramped and suffocating, the air thick with the scent of oil and metal. The generator sat in the center of the room, its mechanical hum vibrating through the floor. Kasai approached it cautiously, scanning the control panel for anything that might shut it down.

"I've got an idea," Riley whispered, pulling a small bundle of wires from the wall. "Help me with this."

Together, they worked quickly, their fingers moving with shaky precision. Kasai's knowledge of machines was limited, but Riley seemed to know what she was doing. Within minutes, they had the wires exposed, ready to cut the power.

"Ready?" Riley asked, her eyes gleaming in the dim light.

Kasai took a deep breath and nodded. "Do it."

Riley severed the wires with a sharp snap, and the generator sputtered before falling silent. The lights outside flickered and died, plunging the compound into darkness.

For a moment, there was only silence.

Then chaos erupted.

Shouts echoed through the night as the guards scrambled to react, their flashlights cutting through the darkness like frantic fireflies. Gunshots rang out, sharp and jarring, and Kasai's heart lurched.

"Go!" Riley hissed, pulling Kasai toward the door.

They slipped back into the shadows, weaving through the confusion as the guards fired blindly into the night. Kasai's lungs burned with every breath, her side screaming in protest, but she didn't slow down.

They reached the others just as Elara led them toward the now-unlit warehouse, her blade flashing in the moonlight.

"You did it," Elara whispered, her eyes filled with both relief and urgency. "Now let's get those people out."

Kasai nodded, pushing down the exhaustion as they moved toward the warehouse entrance. The guards were still distracted, their shouts and gunfire echoing through the compound, but Kasai knew it wouldn't last.

They slipped inside the warehouse, the darkness swallowing them whole. The air was thick with the stench of sweat and fear, and Kasai could hear the faint sobs of the prisoners echoing through the cavernous space.

Elara led them through the maze of crates and machinery, her movements swift and silent. They reached the holding area—a series of makeshift cages constructed from chain-link fencing and barbed wire. The prisoners huddled inside, their faces pale and hollow, their eyes wide with terror.

Kasai's heart clenched as she scanned the faces, searching for her mom. But there was no sign of her.

"Get them out," Elara ordered, her voice low but firm.

They worked quickly, using their tools to pry open the locks and cut through the chains. The prisoners stumbled out, their movements sluggish and hesitant, as if they couldn't believe they were free.

"Go!" Elara urged, guiding them toward the exit. "Head for

the east gate. We've got a path cleared."

Kasai helped a young woman to her feet, her heart aching at the woman's vacant expression. How many more people have they taken?

As the last of the prisoners fled into the night, Elara turned to Kasai and the others. "We're not done yet."

Kasai nodded, her grip tightening on her wrench. They might have saved these people, but the fight was far from over.

And Kasai wasn't leaving until she found her mom.

53 hours left.

The warehouse echoed with the sound of footsteps—prisoners stumbling toward freedom, guards shouting in confusion, and the faint, guttural groans of the infected somewhere in the distance. Kasai's heart pounded in her chest, her muscles screaming in protest as she moved through the darkened space, helping the last of the survivors out of their cages.

The flickering emergency lights cast long, distorted shadows across the walls, making everything feel surreal, like a nightmare she couldn't wake from. But the cold weight of the wrench in her hand and the burning pain in her side reminded her that this was all too real.

"Kasai!" Elara's voice cut through the chaos, sharp and commanding. She was at the far end of the warehouse, waving Kasai over. "We need to move—now!"

Kasai gave a final glance around the room, her eyes scanning the faces of the freed prisoners one last time. She's not here. The realization hit her like a punch to the gut, but there was no time to dwell on it. She forced down the rising tide of fear and disappointment, tightening her grip on her wrench as she sprinted toward Elara.

Riley and Milo were already at the exit, guiding the freed prisoners through a broken side door that led out to the narrow alleys beyond the compound. Caleb was helping Emma and Lucy climb over a stack of crates, his face pale with exhaustion but his movements steady. Sarah and Jason followed close behind, their eyes darting nervously to every shadow.

Kasai reached Elara's side just as a gunshot rang out, the bullet whizzing past her ear and embedding itself in the wall with a sharp thunk. She ducked instinctively, her heart leaping into her throat.

"They've regrouped!" Riley shouted from the doorway, her knife flashing in the dim light. "We need to go!"

Elara grabbed Kasai's arm, pulling her toward the exit. "Move!"

They bolted through the door and into the night, the cool air hitting Kasai's face like a slap. The alley was narrow anddark, the towering buildings on either side closing in like a vice. The freed prisoners stumbled ahead of them, their movements slow and disoriented, but fear gave them strength. They knew what was behind them, and none of them wanted to go back.

Kasai could hear the guards shouting behind them, their footsteps pounding against the concrete as they gave chase. The sharp crack of gunfire echoed through the alley, bullets ricocheting off the walls and sending sparks into the darkness.

"We need to split up!" Elara shouted over the noise, her voice hoarse but unwavering. "They can't follow all of us!"

Kasai's heart clenched at the thought of separating, but she knew Elara was right. It was their only chance.

"I'll take the left with Milo and Caleb!" Riley called out, already pulling the younger boy toward a side street. "Kasai, go with Elara!"

Kasai barely had time to nod before Elara grabbed her arm again, yanking her down a different path. They moved through the labyrinth of alleys like shadows, weaving between broken fences and abandoned cars, the sounds of the city's chaos fading behind them.

They didn't stop running until they reached the edge of the industrial district, where the crumbling buildings gave way to an overgrown park. The trees were skeletal, their bare branches clawing at the sky, and the ground was littered with debris—remnants of a world that no longer existed.

Elara finally slowed, her chest heaving as she pulled Kasai into the cover of an old, rusted playground. They crouched behind a toppled slide, the metal cold against their backs, as they caught their breath.

For a long moment, the only sound was the ragged rasp of their breathing.

Kasai's mind raced, the adrenaline still coursing through her veins. "Do you think the others made it?" she whispered, her voice barely audible.

Elara nodded, though her eyes were clouded with worry. "Riley knows how to handle herself. They'll be okay."

Kasai wanted to believe that, but doubt gnawed at the edges of her mind. They'd lost too many people already, and the thought of losing anyone else was unbearable.

Elara turned to her, her expression softening. "You did good back there."

Kasai shook her head, frustration bubbling to the surface. "But she wasn't there. My mom..." Her voice broke, and she clenched her jaw to keep the tears at bay. "I thought she might be, but she wasn't."

Elara's hand rested gently on Kasai's shoulder. "We'll find her. We're not giving up."

Kasai nodded, swallowing hard against the lump in her throat. She wanted to believe Elara, but with every passing hour, hope felt like it was slipping further out of reach.

The faint sound of footsteps snapped them both to attention.

Elara's hand went to her blade, her eyes narrowing as she scanned the darkness. Kasai gripped her wrench tighter, her heart pounding in her chest.

The footsteps grew louder, and closer until a familiar voice called out softly from the shadows.

"Kasai? Elara?"

It was Milo.

Relief washed over Kasai like a wave as Milo emerged from the darkness, followed closely by Riley, Caleb, and the others. They were battered and exhausted, but alive.

Kasai rushed forward, pulling Milo into a tight hug despite the pain in her side. "You made it," she whispered, her voice thick with emotion.

Milo clung to her, his small body trembling. "I thought we lost you."

Kasai pulled back just enough to look at him, her heart swelling with pride. "Not a chance."

Riley approached, her eyes scanning the group. "We lost them in the alleys. But they'll be looking for us."

Elara nodded, her expression grim. "We can't stay here."

They moved deeper into the park, finding shelter in the hollowed-out remains of an old maintenance shed. The group huddled together for warmth, the night pressing in around them like a suffocating blanket.

Kasai sat with her back against the wall, her eyes drifting to the stars visible through the broken roof. The sky seemed so vast, so indifferent to the chaos below.

Elara's voice broke the silence. "We keep moving east at dawn. The farther we get from the city, the better our chances."

Kasai nodded, the weight of exhaustion settling over her like lead. But beneath the fatigue, a spark of determination burned bright.

They weren't just running anymore. They were fighting.

For survival.

For each other.

For the chance to find those they'd lost.

Kasai closed her eyes, letting the sounds of the night lull her into a restless sleep.

They were still alive.

And as long as they were breathing, they had a chance.

52 hours left.

Chapter 7
The Long Road East

The first rays of dawn painted the sky in muted shades of gray and pink, casting a soft glow over the skeletal trees of the overgrown park. The world felt eerily still as if the chaos of the past days had been nothing but a bad dream. But the ache in Kasai's side and the tension in her chest reminded her that the nightmare was far from over.

She stirred from her restless sleep, her body stiff from the cold and the hard ground beneath her. The maintenance shed had provided some shelter, but the chill of the night had seeped into her bones, leaving her feeling more exhausted than when they'd first collapsed there.

Milo was curled up beside her, his breathing steady but shallow. He clutched his baseball bat even in sleep, his smallhands wrapped tightly around the worn handle like it was the only thing tethering him to reality. Kasai reached out and gently brushed a strand of hair from his face, her heart aching at how young he looked in the dim light. Too young for this.But then again, they all were.

Elara was already awake, sitting near the entrance of the shed with her blade resting across her knees. Her eyes were sharp and alert, scanning the horizon for any sign of movement. She'd probably been awake most of the night, keeping watch while the rest of them tried to snatch a few precious hours of sleep. Kasai admired her strength, but she also worried about how much longer any of them could keep going like this.

Riley stirred next, stretching with a soft groan before sitting up and rubbing the sleep from her eyes. She caught Kasai's gaze and gave a tired nod. No words were needed. They both knew what the day ahead would bring.

Elara's voice broke the morning silence, low but firm. "We move in ten."

The words were met with groans and murmurs from the others as they roused themselves from sleep. Caleb gently shook Emma and Lucy awake, murmuring soft reassurances as the girls blinked blearily at the rising sun. Sarah and Jason gathered their things in silence, their faces pale but determined.

Kasai forced herself to her feet, wincing as a sharp jolt of pain shot through her side. The wound wasn't deep, but it was enough to slow her down. She gritted her teeth and pushed the pain aside. There was no room for weakness—not now.

They moved quickly, packing up what little supplies they had left. The granola bars and bottled water they'd scavenged were running dangerously low, and the realization gnawed at Kasai's mind like a persistent itch. We need to find more soon. But supplies weren't their only concern. The soldiers and raiders would still be hunting them, and the infected were a constant, looming threat.

Elara led them out of the park and back onto the crumbling streets, heading east toward the city's outskirts. The goal was simple: get as far away from the city as possible, and find safety in the rural areas where the infected—and the soldiers—might be fewer. But nothing felt simple anymore.

The sun climbed higher in the sky as they moved, the weak warmth doing little to chase away the cold that had settled into Kasai's bones. The streets were eerily quiet, the only sounds were their footsteps on the cracked pavement and the occasional rustle of wind through the empty buildings. It was unsettling like the city itself was holding its breath, waiting for the next wave of horror to crash over them.

They passed through neighborhoods that had once been bustling with life—now nothing more than hollow shells of what had been. Burned-out cars lined the streets, their charred frames twisted and blackened. Houses stood with doors hanging off their hinges, windows shattered, and furniture strewn across the lawns like the remnants of a violent storm.

At one point, they passed a playground, its swings swaying gently in the breeze, the rusted chains creaking with an almost mournful sound. Kasai's chest tightened at the sight. It was a stark reminder of the world they'd lost, the innocence that had been ripped away.

Milo's voice broke the heavy silence. "Do you think... do you think it'll ever go back to how it was?"

Kasai glanced at him, her heart aching at the hope in his voice. She wanted to tell him yes, that everything would be okay, that the world would heal and they'd all go back to their normal lives. But she couldn't lie to him—not after everything they'd seen.

"I don't know," she said quietly. "But we'll keep fighting for it."

Milo nodded, his grip tightening on his bat. It wasn't the answer he wanted, but it was the truth.

They continued on, the hours stretching out like an endless road. The sun climbed higher, casting harsh shadows across the landscape, but Kasai barely noticed. Her mind was focused on each step, each breath, each beat of her heart. Keep moving. Don't stop. Don't think about what you've lost.

But it was impossible not to think about her mom.

The image of her mother's face haunted her thoughts—the warm smile, the gentle eyes. She clung to the hope that her mom was still out there somewhere, fighting to survive just like they were. I'll find you. I promise.

As the afternoon wore on, they reached the edge of the city, where the urban sprawl gave way to fields and forests. The air felt different here—fresher, cleaner—but the tension in Kasai's chest didn't ease. The danger wasn't behind them. It was everywhere.

Elara called for a break near an old gas station, its sign swinging lazily in the breeze, the letters faded and cracked. They slipped inside, moving cautiously through the dusty aisles, searching for anything useful. Most of the shelves were bare, but Riley managed to find a few cans of food and a half-empty box of crackers.

Kasai slumped against the counter, her body aching from the day's journey. Milo sat beside her, his eyes heavy with exhaustion, but he didn't complain. None of them did. Complaining wouldn't change anything.

Elara gathered them together after they'd eaten, her eyes scanning the horizon through the broken windows. "We'll camp here for the night," she said quietly. "It's too dangerous to move after dark."

Kasai nodded, though the thought of staying in one place made her uneasy. But Elara was right. Traveling at night was a death sentence.

As the sun dipped below the horizon, casting the sky in deep shades of orange and purple, they settled in for the night. The gas station was small and cramped, but it provided shelter from the cold wind. They took turns keeping watch, the hours dragging on in tense silence.

Kasai's turn came just after midnight. She sat near the window, her wrench resting across her lap, her eyes scanning the darkness outside. The night was quiet, too quiet, and every shadow seemed to shift and move in the corner of her vision.

Her mind drifted back to the warehouse, to the faces of the prisoners they'd freed. She wondered where they were now and if they'd made it out of the city safely. And she wondered about her mom. Are you out there? Are you safe?

A faint sound pulled her from her thoughts—a soft shuffle, barely audible over the wind. Kasai's heart leaped into her throat as she strained to hear, her grip tightening on her wrench.

The sound came again, closer this time.

She turned, her eyes scanning the dark interior of the gas station.

A shadow moved near the entrance.

Kasai's breath caught in her throat.

"Elara," she whispered, her voice trembling. "Someone's here."

Elara was on her feet in an instant, her blade drawn, eyes sharp and focused. Riley moved to Kasai's side, her knife glinting in the dim light. The others stirred, their fear palpable in the cold air.

The door creaked open.

And a figure stepped inside.

Kasai's heart stopped.

It was a woman—her face pale and gaunt, her clothes torn and dirty. But Kasai would recognize those eyes anywhere.

"Mom?"

The woman's eyes widened, and for a brief, heart-stopping moment, Kasai thought it was really her.

But then the woman smiled—a twisted, unnatural smile that sent a chill down Kasai's spine.

It wasn't her mom.

It was something else.

The infected woman let out a guttural, inhuman scream, and the world erupted into chaos.

51 hours left.

The inhuman scream ripped through the gas station like a knife, freezing Kasai where she stood. Her mind registered the horrific sound before her body could react—guttural and raw, vibrating through the cold air like a warning bell. The woman at the entrance wasn't her mother. The hollow, sunken eyes, the twisted grin, and the unnatural way she stood—it was all wrong. She's one of them.

"Move!" Elara's voice snapped Kasai out of her daze, sharp and commanding.

The infected woman lunged forward, her limbs jerking in that terrifying, erratic way Kasai had come to recognize. Kasai's heart pounded in her chest, her fingers tightening around the wrench in her hand. She barely had time to react before Riley darted in front of her, her knife flashing in the dim light.

With one swift motion, Riley plunged the blade into the infected woman's neck, twisting it sharply before yanking it free. The woman crumpled to the floor, a strangled gurgle escaping her lips. But the relief was short-lived.

More shuffling sounds echoed from outside.

Kasai's breath hitched. There's more.

"They heard her," Elara whispered, her eyes flicking toward the boarded windows. "We've got to get out of here. Now."

Milo scrambled to his feet, clutching his baseball bat so tightly his knuckles turned white. Caleb gathered Emma and Lucy in his arms, their wide, terrified eyes darting around the room. Sarah and Jason stood close by, their faces pale with fear.

Kasai's heart raced as she scanned the gas station for an escape route. The front door was no longer an option—it would lead them straight into the infected. The back, maybe? There has to be another way.

"Back door!" Riley hissed, already moving toward the storage room.

Kasai followed, her side screaming in protest with every step. The pain was sharp and constant now, but she pushed it aside, focusing on survival. They slipped into the dark storage room, the faint smell of gasoline and mold clinging to the air.

Elara kicked open the rusted back door, the hinges groaning in protest. The cold night air rushed in, carrying with it the distant sounds of the infected. Kasai felt the chill seep into her bones, but she didn't stop moving.

They poured out into the alley behind the gas station, the moonlight casting long shadows on the cracked pavement. Kasai could hear them now—the infected, closing in from all sides. Their guttural moans echoed off the walls, growing louder with every passing second.

"We need to split up," Elara said, her voice low but firm. "We'll meet at the old water tower on the hill. It's east of here— just keep moving."

Kasai's stomach twisted at the thought of separating again,

but she knew Elara was right. Splitting up would give them a better chance of slipping past the infected.

"I'm with you," Milo whispered, his voice trembling but determined.

Kasai nodded, her heart swelling with pride. She grabbed his hand, squeezing it tightly. "Stay close."

Riley and Elara led Caleb, Sarah, and the kids down one alley, while Kasai and Milo darted down another, the sounds of the infected fading behind them as they moved deeper into the maze of dark streets.

The cold night air burned Kasai's lungs as they ran, her heart pounding in rhythm with her footsteps. The city felt like a living thing now—watching, waiting, hunting. Every shadow seemed to shift, every distant sound a potential threat.

They weaved through alleys and backstreets, avoiding the main roads where the infected were more likely to gather. But the city was alive with their presence. Kasai could hear them everywhere—their guttural cries, the shuffle of their broken limbs against the pavement.

After what felt like an eternity, they ducked into an old laundromat, the glass windows shattered and the machines covered in layers of dust. Kasai slumped against one of the washing machines, her chest heaving as she tried to catch her breath.

Milo crouched beside her, his eyes wide and fearful. "Do you think the others made it?"

Kasai swallowed hard, forcing herself to stay calm. Elara's smart. Riley's tough. They'll make it. She had to believe that. It was the only thing keeping her going.

"They'll be at the water tower," she whispered, her voice hoarse. "We just have to get there."

Milo nodded, his grip tightening on his bat. They rested for only a few minutes, just long enough for their breathing to steady, before slipping back into the night.

The city grew quieter as they moved farther east, the buildings giving way to open fields and patches of forest. But the silence wasn't comforting. It was the kind of silence that pressed in on you, heavy and suffocating, filled with the promise of danger.

Kasai's body screamed with every step, her side throbbing with pain, but she didn't slow down. She couldn't. They were so close.

They reached the base of the hill just as the first light of dawn began to creep over the horizon. The old water tower loomed above them, its rusted frame silhouetted against the pale sky.

Kasai's heart leaped at the sight. We made it.

But the relief was short-lived.

As they approached the tower, Kasai spotted movement at the top of the hill. Her heart stopped.

It wasn't Elara or Riley.

It was soldiers.

A small group of them, armed and alert, their uniforms marked with the same symbols Kasai had seen on the convoy trucks. They were setting up a perimeter around the tower, their eyes scanning the horizon for any sign of movement.

Kasai ducked behind a tree, pulling Milo down with her. Her mind raced, trying to make sense of what she was seeing.

Why are they here?

Were they using the water tower as another holding site? A lookout? She didn't know, but one thing was clear—they couldn't walk into this without a plan.

Milo's voice was barely a whisper. "What do we do?"

Kasai stared at the soldiers, her heart pounding in her chest. She thought of Elara, Riley, Caleb, and the kids. They were out there somewhere, trying to make it to this very spot. If they stumbled into the soldiers without knowing, they'd be caught— or worse.

"We wait," Kasai whispered, her mind already racing through possibilities. "We figure out how many there are. We find a way around them."

But as they crouched in the shadows, watching the soldiers move with ruthless efficiency, Kasai felt a cold, sinking feeling settled in her chest.

This wasn't just about survival anymore.

They were in the heart of something much bigger—something

far more dangerous.

And the clock was still ticking.

50 hours left.

Kasai's breath came in shallow bursts as she crouched behind the gnarled tree trunk, the rough bark biting into her back. The soldiers were moving with eerie precision, their boots crunching against the frost-covered ground as they secured the perimeter around the water tower. Each one was armed with military-grade rifles, their faces hidden beneath helmets and dark visors that reflected the pale morning light.

What are they doing here? Kasai's mind raced. The water tower wasn't just a random landmark—it had to mean something. Maybe it was another holding site like the warehouse, or maybe something worse. Whatever it was, they couldn't just walk into it blindly.

Beside her, Milo shifted, his small frame pressed tightly against the base of the tree. His eyes were wide with fear, but there was a spark of determination there too. He wasn't the same scared kid she'd met on that rooftop. He'd fought, survived, and grown stronger with every day. But Kasai could see the exhaustion weighing on him, the same exhaustion she felt in every muscle, every bone.

"What do we do now?" Milo whispered, his voice barely audible over the wind rustling through the trees.

Kasai swallowed hard, her mind working through the options. They could wait and hope the soldiers moved on, but there was no guarantee. And if Elara and the others were on their way here, they could walk straight into an ambush.

"We need to get closer," she whispered back, her grip tightening on the wrench in her hand. "See how many there are, what they're guarding."

Milo's eyes darted back to the soldiers, then to Kasai. He nodded, his jaw set with grim determination. "Okay."

They crept along the tree line, keeping low and moving as silently as possible. Kasai winced with every step, her side burning with each breath, but she pushed the pain aside. She had to. They followed the curve of the hill, using the sparse cover of the trees and underbrush to stay hidden.

As they neared the water tower, Kasai could see more clearly. There were at least six soldiers—maybe more—patrolling the area. But what caught her attention wasn't just the soldiers. It was the truck parked near the base of the tower. Unlikethe convoy trucks they'd seen before, this one was smaller but heavily armored. Its back doors were slightly ajar, revealing glimpses of crates and strange equipment inside.

Kasai's heart pounded harder. What the hell is going on?

She motioned for Milo to stay back as she edged closer, her body pressed flat against the ground. The cold dirt seeped into her clothes, but she barely noticed. Every sense was focused on the soldiers' movements, timing her approach with their patrols.

She was close enough now to hear snippets of their conversation—low, clipped voices through the static of their radios.

"...transport arriving within the hour."

"...secure the perimeter. No one gets through."

Kasai's pulse quickened. Transport? Were they bringing more prisoners? Supplies? Or something worse?

She was about to retreat when she heard a sound that froze her blood.

A scream.

Faint, muffled—but unmistakable.

It was coming from the truck.

Kasai's heart lurched. Someone was in there—alive. What are they doing to them?

She crawled back to Milo, her mind racing. When she reached him, his eyes were wide, his face pale.

"I heard it," he whispered, his voice trembling. "Someone's in that truck."

Kasai nodded, her stomach twisting. "We can't leave them."

"But how do we get past the guards?" Milo's voice wavered, but there was a fierce determination behind it. He wanted to fight just as much as she did.

Kasai bit her lip, thinking. They were outnumbered and outgunned. A direct confrontation would be suicide. But maybe they didn't need to fight head-on.

She glanced at the truck, and then at the trees surrounding them. A plan began to form in her mind—risky, dangerous, but it was the only chance they had.

"We need a distraction," she said quietly. "Something to draw them away from the truck."

Milo's brow furrowed. "Like what?"

Kasai scanned the area, her eyes landing on a small, rusted metal shed near the edge of the clearing. It was old, probably abandoned long before the outbreak, but it was close enough to the soldiers' perimeter that a loud noise from there might pull them away from the truck.

"We'll set a fire," she whispered. "Smoke, noise—it'll pull them away long enough for us to get inside the truck."

Milo's eyes widened, but he nodded. "Okay."

They moved quickly, gathering dry brush and leaves from the forest floor and piling them near the shed. Kasai found an old, broken gas can near the back of the shed, the faint smell of gasoline still lingering inside. She poured what little was left over the pile, her hands trembling slightly.

Milo pulled out the box of matches they'd found in the convenience store. His hands shook as he struck one, the tiny flame flickering in the wind. He hesitated for a moment, then dropped it onto the pile.

The fire caught quickly, the dry leaves and brush igniting with a sharp crackle. Smoke billowed into the air, thick and black, curling up toward the sky.

"Let's go," Kasai hissed, grabbing Milo's arm and pulling him back toward the truck.

The soldiers' shouts echoed through the clearing as they spotted the smoke. Kasai watched from the shadows as they moved toward the fire, rifles raised, their attention focused on the growing blaze.

Now or never.

Kasai and Milo sprinted toward the truck, their footsteps

muffled against the soft dirt. Kasai's heart pounded in her chest, her mind racing with fear and adrenaline. They reached the truck in seconds, and Kasai yanked the door open, her breath hitching in her throat.

Inside, huddled against the wall, was a young woman—no older than Kasai—her wrists bound with plastic ties, her face bruised and bloodied. Her eyes widened in shock and fear as Kasai stepped inside.

"It's okay," Kasai whispered, her voice shaking. "We're here to help."

The woman stared at her for a moment, then nodded weakly. Kasai pulled out the small knife Riley had given her and quickly cut through the ties.

"We need to move," Milo whispered urgently from the door. "They'll be back any second."

Kasai helped the woman to her feet, supporting her weight as they slipped out of the truck. The fire was still burning, but the soldiers were starting to realize it was a distraction. Shouts rang out as they spotted Kasai and Milo, and the sharp crack of gunfire split the air.

"Run!" Kasai screamed, her voice raw with fear.

They sprinted back toward the trees, bullets whizzing past them, kicking up dirt and debris. Kasai's legs burned, her lungs screamed, but she didn't stop. She couldn't.

They reached the cover of the trees, the dense underbrush shielding them from view. They didn't stop running until the soldiers' shouts faded into the distance, replaced by the steady thrum of their own racing hearts.

When they finally collapsed behind a fallen tree, gasping for breath, Kasai turned to the woman they'd rescued.

"Who are you?" Kasai whispered, her voice barely audible.

The woman looked at her, her eyes filled with a mix of fear and relief.

"My name's Ava," she said quietly. "And you don't know what you've gotten yourselves into."

Kasai's heart pounded in her chest. She didn't know what Ava meant, but one thing was clear.

This was far from over.

49 hours left.

Kasai's breath came in ragged gasps as she leaned against the fallen tree, her chest heaving from the sprint. Milo sat beside her, his face flushed and damp with sweat, but his grip on his bat never wavered. Between them, Ava huddled close, her eyes darting nervously to every shadow as if expecting the soldiers to burst through the trees at any moment.

The forest was silent now, except for the faint crackle of the fire they'd left behind and the distant shouts of confused soldiers. The adrenaline still surged through Kasai's veins, but her mind was sharp, locked onto Ava's last words.

"You don't know what you've gotten yourselves into."

Kasai turned to her, heart pounding. "What do you mean? What's going on at that tower?"

Ava hesitated, her eyes flicking between Kasai and Milo. Her face was pale, streaked with dirt and dried blood, but there was something in her eyes—fear, yes, but also knowledge. Something heavy.

"They're not just rounding people up," Ava whispered, her voice barely audible over the rustling of the leaves. "They're experimenting... trying to control the infected. But it's more than that now." She shivered, pulling her arms around her knees. "They're using people. Injecting them with... something. Trying to turn them, but not like the infected you've seen. These... these are worse."

Kasai felt her stomach twist. She remembered the blank stares of the people in the community center gym, the unnatural way they moved in unison. It wasn't just random chaos—the soldiers were trying to control the outbreak, to weaponize it.

And they were willing to sacrifice anyone to do it.

Milo's voice was a whisper. "Why?"

Ava shook her head, her eyes haunted. "I don't know. But they're moving everyone to a new site. That water tower is just a checkpoint." She glanced back toward the hill, her voice dropping even lower. "They're heading somewhere deeper in the woods. A facility. They call it 'The Nest.'"

Kasai's pulse quickened. The Nest. The name alone sent a chill down her spine. Whatever was happening there, it was worse than anything they'd seen so far.

"We need to warn the others," Kasai said, pushing herself to her feet despite the screaming protest from her side. "Elara, Riley—they're heading here. We can't let them walk into this."

Ava's hand shot out, grabbing Kasai's wrist. Her grip was surprisingly strong for someone who looked so fragile. "You don't understand," she hissed. "They're not just soldiers. They have people out there—spies. They know where survivors are hiding. That's how they keep finding groups like ours." Her voice trembled. "That's how they found me."

Kasai's heart sank. Spies. The idea that someone could be feeding information to the soldiers made her skin crawl. She thought of everyone she'd met along the way—the other survivors they'd helped, the people they'd lost. Could someone have betrayed them?

Milo shifted uncomfortably, his eyes wide with fear. "What if they're watching us right now?"

Kasai shook her head, trying to keep her own fear at bay. "We can't think like that. We trust each other, or we don't make it."

But even as she said it, doubt gnawed at the edges of her mind. Trust had become a fragile currency in this world, and every betrayal they'd faced had chipped away at what little remained.

"We need to move," Kasai said, glancing toward the rising sun. "We can't stay here."

Ava nodded, but her eyes remained wary. "If we're going to find your friends, we need to circle around the tower. There's an old maintenance road that leads east. It's hidden, but it should keep us out of sight."

Kasai helped Milo to his feet, wincing as her side flared with pain. She clenched her jaw and nodded. "Lead the way."

They moved quickly, slipping through the dense underbrush, keeping low, and avoiding the main paths. Kasai's heart raced with every step, her ears straining for any sound of pursuit. The forest felt alive, each rustle of leaves or snap of a twig setting her nerves on edge.

They followed Ava through a narrow, overgrown trail, the trees closing in around them like skeletal fingers. The path twisted and turned, weaving deeper into the forest, until the sounds of the soldiers and the burning fire were nothing more than distant echoes.

After what felt like hours, they emerged into a small clearing, where the remnants of an old maintenance shack stood crumbling in the center. The roof had partially collapsed, and vines crept up the walls, but it provided cover—and a moment to breathe.

Kasai slumped against the side of the shack, her chest heaving. Milo sat beside her, his face pale and drawn, but his eyes were alert. Ava sat near the edge of the clearing, her gaze constantly scanning the trees.

Kasai turned to Milo, her voice low. "We'll find Elara and the others. We have to."

Milo nodded, his jaw set with determination. "We will."

But before Kasai could say more, Ava froze, her body tense.

"Do you hear that?" she whispered.

Kasai strained her ears, her heart pounding in her chest. At first, she heard nothing but the wind rustling through the leaves. But then—faint, almost imperceptible—the sound of footsteps. Multiple footsteps.

They were close.

Kasai's blood ran cold. They found us.

Ava darted back toward them, her eyes wide with panic. "We have to move. Now."

But it was too late.

Figures emerged from the trees—four soldiers, their rifles raised, visors gleaming in the dim light. They moved with practiced precision, fanning out to surround the clearing.

Kasai's mind raced. We're trapped.

One of the soldiers stepped forward, his voice amplified by a radio attached to his chest. "Drop your weapons. Hands where we can see them."

Kasai's grip tightened on her wrench. She could feel Milo

trembling beside her, but he didn't let go of his bat. Ava stood rigid, her eyes darting between the soldiers and Kasai.

For a moment, no one moved.

Then Kasai saw it.

A flicker of recognition in one of the soldier's eyes—the smallest hesitation, but enough to make her heart skip a beat. *I know him.*

She squinted, her mind racing through the fog of fear and exhaustion, trying to place his face. And then it hit her.

It was Daniel.

The soldier they thought Milo had killed at the warehouse.

But he wasn't dead. And now he was standing in front of them, alive and very much a threat.

Daniel's lips curled into a cruel smile beneath his visor. "Miss me?"

Kasai's blood boiled. *How?* She remembered Milo's trembling hands, the gunshot echoing through the warehouse. She'd seen Daniel fall, seen the blood.

But he was here.

And that meant they were in more danger than she'd ever imagined.

Without thinking, Kasai lunged forward, swinging her wrench with everything she had. But Daniel was faster. He sidestepped her attack with ease, slamming the butt of his rifle into her injured side.

Pain exploded through her body, and she crumpled to the ground, gasping for breath.

"Kasai!" Milo screamed, rushing toward her.

But Daniel grabbed him by the collar, yanking him off his feet. "Not so fast, kid."

Ava tried to run, but one of the other soldiers tackled her, pinning her to the ground.

Kasai struggled to rise, her vision blurring from the pain. But Daniel knelt beside her, pressing the cold barrel of his rifle against her forehead.

"You should've stayed hidden," he whispered, his voice low and menacing. "But now? Now you're going to see what The Nest is really about."

Kasai's heart pounded in her chest, her mind racing.

This isn't over.

She clenched her jaw, staring into Daniel's cold, unfeeling eyes.

Not by a long shot.

48 hours left.

Kasai's heartbeat roared in her ears as Daniel's rifle pressed cold and unyielding against her forehead. Every instinct screamed at her to fight, to do something, but the searing pain in her side made even breathing a challenge. She could see Milo struggling in Daniel's grip, his small fists pounding against the soldier's armored chest, his face red with frustration and fear.

But Daniel wasn't even flinching.

"Let him go!" Kasai gasped, her voice strained, but her glare burned with defiance.

Daniel chuckled, the sound low and cruel. "I could've killed you at the warehouse. Should've, maybe." His eyes gleamed behind the visor. "But this is better. Now I get to deliver you personally."

Kasai's mind raced. Deliver us? To who? She could still hear Ava struggling under the weight of another soldier, her muffled cries cutting through the tense air. The other two soldiers were scanning the perimeter, their rifles raised, ready for any sign of movement.

They're not expecting an attack.

A sudden idea sparked in Kasai's mind—a dangerous, reckless one, but it was all they had. She glanced at Milo, who caught her look, his frantic eyes locking onto hers. For a moment, everything around them seemed to fade, and there was only the unspoken understanding between them.

Kasai mouthed two words: Be ready.

With every ounce of strength she had left, Kasai jerked her head to the side, wrenching herself away from the rifle's barrel. The motion sent a fresh wave of agony through her injured side, but she didn't care. She had one chance.

At the same time, Milo sank his teeth into Daniel's wrist.

Daniel let out a surprised, enraged shout and instinctively

loosened his grip. Milo wrenched free, scrambling out of reach as Kasai swung her wrench upward with all her strength, catching Daniel's jaw with a sickening crack. The soldier staggered back, clutching his face, his rifle clattering to the ground.

"Milo, run!" Kasai screamed, her voice raw.

But Milo didn't run. He grabbed Daniel's fallen rifle, his hands trembling but determined, and swung it like a bat at the nearest soldier pinning Ava to the ground.

The impact sent the soldier sprawling, giving Ava just enough room to scramble free. She didn't hesitate—grabbing a large rock from the ground and slamming it into the soldier's head with a desperate, feral cry.

Kasai forced herself to her feet, her vision swimming, but there was no time to recover. One of the other soldiers raised his rifle toward Milo, his finger tightening on the trigger.

No.

Kasai didn't think—she moved. She threw her wrench with all the force she could muster, the metal spinning through the air before it slammed into the soldier's temple. The man dropped like a stone, his rifle firing harmlessly into the ground.

For a moment, there was silence.

Then chaos.

Daniel roared in fury, lunging at Kasai, his face twisted with rage, but Ava was faster. She tackled him from the side, sending them both crashing to the ground. They rolled in the dirt, grappling for control, Ava's rock raised high as Daniel fought to reach his sidearm.

Milo rushed to Kasai's side, his wide eyes filled with panic. "We have to help her!"

Kasai's body screamed in protest, but she nodded, gritting her teeth against the pain. Together, they charged toward Ava and Daniel, but before they could reach them, a single gunshot echoed through the forest.

Ava froze.

Daniel's body went limp beneath her, a dark stain spreading across his chest.

Kasai's heart pounded in her chest as she looked up to see

Elara standing at the edge of the clearing, her pistol still raised, smoke curling from the barrel. Riley stood beside her, her knife dripping with fresh blood, and Caleb was just behind them, his arms wrapped tightly around Emma and Lucy, shielding them from the scene.

For a moment, no one spoke.

Then Elara lowered her weapon, her sharp eyes locking onto Kasai's.

"You didn't think we'd leave you behind, did you?" she said, her voice calm but laced with steel.

Relief washed over Kasai, so overwhelming that her knees nearly buckled beneath her. But there was no time for tears or gratitude.

"We need to move," Elara continued, her eyes flicking to the remaining soldier—unconscious but still breathing. "More will come when they hear the gunfire."

Kasai nodded, wincing as she straightened up. "They're taking people to a place called The Nest," she said, her voice hoarse. "That's where they're experimenting on them."

Elara's expression darkened. "Then that's where we're going."

Riley raised an eyebrow. "Are you serious? We barely made it out of this mess alive."

Elara didn't flinch. "We can't leave those people. If we don't stop them, no one will."

Kasai felt a swell of determination rise in her chest. As terrifying as it was, Elara was right. They couldn't turn back now.

"We'll find it," Ava said quietly, her voice steady despite the tremor in her hands. "I know the way."

Elara nodded once. "Then let's move."

They left the clearing behind, slipping deeper into the forest, the weight of their mission settling over them like a second skin. Every step forward felt heavier, not just from exhaustion, but from the knowledge of what lay ahead.

As they moved, Kasai found herself walking beside Milo, their shoulders brushing with each step. She glanced down at him, seeing the determination etched into his young face, the fear hidden just beneath the surface.

"You were brave back there," she whispered.

Milo shrugged, but a faint smile tugged at the corner of his mouth. "I learned from the best."

Kasai's heart swelled with pride and fear. She didn't want Milo to have to be brave. She wanted him to be safe. But in this world, bravery was the only thing keeping them alive.

As the sun began to set, casting long shadows across the forest floor, they reached the edge of a steep ravine. Ava motioned for them to stop, crouching near the edge and pointing down.

"There," she whispered.

Kasai followed her gaze, her breath catching in her throat.

Nestled deep within the ravine, partially hidden by the dense trees, was a sprawling complex of concrete and steel. Fences topped with barbed wire surrounded the perimeter, and spotlights swept across the grounds in slow, methodical patterns. The faint hum of generators filled the air, accompanied by the distant, haunting screams of the people trapped inside.

The Nest.

Kasai's heart pounded in her chest, a mix of fear and determination swirling within her. This was it—the heart of the nightmare. The place where they'd been turning people into weapons, experimenting on them like lab rats.

Elara crouched beside her, her sharp eyes scanning the complex.

"We go in at dawn," she said quietly. "We'll rest tonight, watch their patterns, and then we hit them hard."

Kasai nodded, her grip tightening on her wrench. She knew the risks. She knew they might not all make it out alive.

But they had to try.

Because this wasn't just about survival anymore.

It was about fighting back.

For the people, they'd lost.

For the ones they still had.

And for the future that was slipping through their fingers.

As the first stars appeared in the darkening sky, Kasai felt a flicker of hope ignite in her chest.

They were still alive.
And as long as they were breathing, they had a chance.
47 hours left

Chapter 8
The Nest

The forest was a living thing at night, breathing in slow, heavy sighs as the wind whispered through the trees. The distant hum of generators from The Nest vibrated through the ground beneath Kasai's feet, a constant, unnerving reminder of what lay ahead. She crouched behind a thick tree trunk at the edge of the ravine, her eyes locked on the sprawling facility below.

Spotlights swept methodically across the perimeter, their beams slicing through the darkness like blades. Guards patrolled the fence line in pairs, their rifles gleaming under the harsh artificial light. Beyond the outer fence, Kasai could see the outlines of low, squat buildings—barracks, maybe, or storage units. But it was the central structure that held her attention: a large, windowless building made of cold, gray concrete. Even from a distance, it radiated menace.

That's where they were keeping the prisoners.

That's where they were conducting the experiments.

Kasai's heart pounded in her chest, her muscles tense despite the cold that seeped through her clothes. Every breath felt heavy like the air itself was pressing down on her. But beneath the fear, a flicker of determination burned bright. They'd made it this far.

They weren't going to stop now.

Elara crouched beside her, her sharp eyes scanning the facility with a calculating intensity. Riley was a few feet away, cleaning her knife with slow, deliberate strokes, while Milo sat quietly at Kasai's other side, his hands wrapped tightly around his baseball bat. Ava leaned against a tree trunk, her face pale in the moonlight but her eyes hard and resolute.

Caleb and the kids were farther back, hidden in the thicker part of the forest. They'd argued about leaving them behind, but Caleb had insisted it was too dangerous for Emma and Lucy to get any closer. He'd promised to keep them safe, to wait for their return.

If they returned.

Elara's voice was a soft whisper, barely audible over the rustling of the leaves. "We've got two options," she said, her eyes never leaving the facility. "We can create a diversion to draw the guards away from the main building, or we can try to sneak in through the maintenance tunnels Ava mentioned."

Kasai glanced at Ava, who nodded grimly. "There's an entrance on the far side of the ravine," she whispered. "It's old, but it should still be accessible. It'll take us under the fence and into the lower levels of the main building."

Riley snorted softly. "And let me guess—those tunnels are probably crawling with infected?"

Ava's lips pressed into a thin line. "Probably."

Silence settled over the group as they weighed their options. Neither plan was safe. Both were filled with risks. But they didn't have a choice.

Kasai swallowed hard, her mind racing. The tunnels would be dangerous, but a full-frontal assault would be suicide. They needed to be smart, to use the element of surprise.

"I say we take the tunnels," Kasai whispered, her voice steady despite the fear gnawing at her edges. "It's risky, but it's our best shot."

Elara nodded, her expression unreadable. "Agreed. We'll move at first light."

They spent the rest of the night in tense silence, taking turns keeping watch while the others rested as best they could. Kasai tried to close her eyes, but sleep wouldn't come. Every time she drifted off, she saw her mother's face—smiling, then screaming, then disappearing into the shadows of The Nest.

When the first light of dawn painted the sky in muted shades of gray and pink, Elara signaled for them to move. They gathered their things quickly and quietly, slipping through the forest like shadows.

The entrance to the maintenance tunnels was hidden beneath a pile of debris at the far side of the ravine. It was little more than a rusted metal hatch, half-buried under dirt and overgrown with vines. Ava knelt beside it, her hands trembling slightly as she pried it open, the hinges groaning in protest.

A foul stench wafted from the dark opening, a mix of mildew, decay, and something far worse. Kasai gagged, covering her mouth with her sleeve, but forced herself to move forward.

One by one, they descended into the darkness, the narrow tunnel walls closing in around them like a vice. The air was thick and damp, every breath tasting of rust and rot. Their footsteps echoed off the metal walls, each sound magnified in the claustrophobic space.

Kasai gripped her wrench tightly, her heart pounding in her chest. The darkness pressed in on her, but she kept moving, following the faint beam of Elara's flashlight as it cut through the gloom.

The tunnels stretched on endlessly, twisting and turning in disorienting patterns. They passed rusted pipes and broken machinery, the walls slick with moisture and grime. Every now and then, Kasai thought she heard something—soft, shuffling sounds, like something moving just out of sight—but when she turned to look, there was nothing there.

They were deep underground when they finally reached a heavy metal door, its surface covered in peeling paint and rust. Ava moved to the front, her hands shaking as she examined the old lock.

"This leads to the lower levels," she whispered. "Once we're in, we'll need to move fast. The labs are on the upper floors, but the cells..." Her voice trailed off, and she didn't finish the sentence.

Kasai didn't need her to. She knew what Ava meant.

Elara nodded, her face set with grim determination. "We're ready."

Ava pried the door open with a loud creak, the sound echoing through the tunnel like a gunshot. For a moment, they all froze, waiting to see if anyone—or anything—had heard them.

Silence.

They slipped through the door and into the lower levels of The Nest.

The air inside was colder, sharper. The fluorescent lights flickered overhead, casting everything in a sickly, greenish hue. The walls were lined with metal doors, some marked with strange symbols, others with numbers that made Kasai's stomach twist.

They moved quickly, sticking to the shadows, their footsteps muffled against the concrete floor. The facility was eerily quiet, but the tension in the air was suffocating. Kasai could feel it pressing down on her with every step.

As they rounded a corner, they found their first sign of life.

A guard.

He was slumped against the wall, his uniform stained with blood, his eyes wide and unseeing. His mouth was frozen in a silent scream, and deep, jagged wounds covered his arms and neck.

Kasai's stomach lurched.

"Something's wrong," Ava whispered, her voice trembling.

Elara knelt beside the body, her eyes narrowing as she examined the wounds. "These aren't from infected," she muttered. "This was something else."

Before Kasai could ask what she meant, a loud, metallic clang echoed through the corridor, followed by a low, guttural growl.

Her blood ran cold.

They weren't alone.

Elara motioned for them to move, her eyes sharp and focused. They slipped deeper into the facility, the sounds of growls and distant screams growing louder with every step.

As they approached another door, Kasai's heart nearly

stopped.

She heard it.

A voice.

Faint, but unmistakable.

"Kasai..."

Her breath caught in her throat. She turned to Ava, who nodded, her eyes wide.

"It's coming from the cells," Ava whispered.

Kasai didn't hesitate. She darted toward the sound, her heart pounding in her chest. The others followed, their footsteps echoing behind her.

They reached a large metal door marked Containment Unit 4. Kasai didn't wait for permission. She slammed the door open, her eyes scanning the dimly lit room.

And there, huddled in the corner of a filthy cell, was her mother.

Kasai's breath hitched. "Mom..."

Her mother looked up, her face pale and gaunt, but her eyes—her eyes—were the same warm brown Kasai remembered.

"Kasai..." her mother whispered, tears streaming down her face. "You found me."

But before Kasai could move, before she could step into the cell, a loud, guttural roar echoed through the corridor behind them.

They weren't safe.

Not yet.

Kasai turned, her heart pounding in her chest.

The real fight was just beginning.

46 hours left.

The roar reverberated through the cold, sterile air of the containment unit, rattling the metal walls and sending a chill down Kasai's spine. It wasn't the guttural growl of an ordinary infected. This was deeper, more primal—wrong.

Kasai's heart pounded so hard she could hear it in her ears, louder even than her ragged breathing. She stood frozen at the threshold of the cell, staring at her mother's gaunt face, her lips trembling with relief and fear.

"Kasai..." her mother whispered again, her voice thin and weak, but it was her. She was alive.

Before Kasai could move, Elara's hand clamped down on her shoulder, pulling her back into the harsh reality of the situation.

"Not yet," Elara hissed, her sharp eyes scanning the corridor. "We've got company."

Another roar echoed, this time closer, followed by the heavy, erratic thud of something massive moving through the halls. The ground seemed to vibrate with each step, and Kasai felt her stomach twist into a knot.

"Riley, lock the door!" Elara barked, pulling Kasai back from the cell.

"But my mom—" Kasai protested, her voice cracking.

"We're not leaving her," Elara snapped. "But if we're dead, it won't matter."

Riley slammed the heavy door shut, jamming a metal rod through the handle to secure it. Kasai's mother let out a weak, desperate cry from inside the cell, but Kasai forced herself to focus. We'll get her out. We have to.

Ava pressed her back against the wall, her face pale as a ghost. "That's not just infected," she whispered, her eyes wide with terror. "That's one of their experiments."

Kasai's blood ran cold. Experiments. She remembered what Ava had said about the soldiers trying to control the infection, to create something more dangerous. They succeeded.

Milo clutched his bat tightly, his knuckles white. "What do we do?"

Elara's eyes darted to a nearby door marked Maintenance Access. "We move. Now."

They sprinted toward the door just as the thing rounded the corner.

Kasai caught only a glimpse of it before Elara shoved her through the maintenance door, but it was enough to haunt her forever.

It had once been human—that much was clear. But now, its body was grotesquely twisted, muscles bulging unnaturally beneath mottled, gray skin. Its face was a grotesque mask of rage, with milky, sightless eyes and a mouth stretched into an inhuman snarl, jagged teeth glinting under the flickering lights. Metal spikes jutted from its arms and spine, remnants of some cruel experiment.

It charged down the hallway, slamming into the walls as it moved, its roars deafening.

Riley slammed the maintenance door shut just as the creature barreled into it, the impact sending a shudder through the walls. The door buckled, but it held—for now.

They bolted down the narrow maintenance tunnel, the echo of the creature's roars following them like a shadow. The air was thick with dust and the sharp scent of rust and chemicals. Pipes lined the walls, some leaking steam that hissed as they passed.

Kasai's mind raced. We need to get back to Mom. We can't leave her. But first, they had to survive.

The tunnel opened into a large utility room filled with old, rusted machinery. Elara motioned for them to stop, her chest heaving as she caught her breath.

"We need a plan," she said, her voice low but steady.

Kasai's pulse raced. "We have to go back. My mom—"

Elara shook her head. "We will. But that thing isn't going to let us just walk in there. We need to figure out how to kill it first."

Ava stepped forward, her face still pale but her eyes sharp. "It's not invincible. They injected them with some kind ofserum—it made them stronger, and faster, but they're still vulnerable. The injection sites... they're weak points."

Kasai frowned. "Injection sites?"

Ava nodded. "They usually inject along the spine or in the neck. If we can hit those spots hard enough, we might be able to take it down."

Riley scoffed. "Great. All we have to do is get close enough to stab it in the back of the neck while it's trying to rip us apart. No problem."

Elara ignored her sarcasm. "We'll need a distraction."

Kasai's mind raced, trying to piece together a plan. "What about the pipes? The ones leaking steam?" She pointed back toward the tunnel. "If we can lure it near one and rupture it, the steam might slow it down or disorient it."

Elara nodded thoughtfully. "It's risky. But it might work."

Milo stepped forward, his grip still tight on his bat. "I'll do it. I'll be the distraction."

Kasai's heart seized. "No, Milo. It's too dangerous."

But Milo's eyes were steady, his jaw set with determination. "I can do it. I'm fast. I'll lead it to the steam, and then you guys can take it down."

Kasai opened her mouth to argue, but Elara cut her off.

"He's right," Elara said softly. "But we'll be right behind him."

Kasai clenched her fists, the fear gnawing at her insides. But there was no other choice. They had to work together if they were going to survive.

Elara outlined the plan quickly. Milo would lure the creature toward the leaky pipes, and when it was close enough, Kasai and Riley would rupture the main valve to release a blast of scalding steam. While the creature was disoriented, Elara and Ava would go to the injection sites.

Kasai felt her heart pounding in her chest as they crept back toward the maintenance door. The creature was still there, its massive body slamming against the metal, each impact sending shudders through the floor.

Milo took a deep breath, his small frame tense but ready. "See you on the other side," he whispered, flashing Kasai a small, brave smile.

Kasai squeezed his hand tightly. "Be careful."

Milo nodded, then darted through the door.

The creature roared, its head snapping toward Milo as he sprinted down the corridor. It let out a deafening snarl and charged after him, the ground trembling with each heavy step.

Kasai and the others followed at a distance, their hearts pounding in time with their footsteps. Milo led the creature toward the leaking pipes, weaving through the corridor with surprising agility.

As Milo reached the spot, he skidded to a stop, waving his arms to keep the creature's attention. "Come on, you ugly freak!" he shouted, his voice echoing off the walls.

Kasai and Riley sprinted to the valve, their hands fumbling with the rusted metal. The creature was almost on top of Milo now, its massive claws swiping through the air.

"Now!" Elara shouted.

Kasai and Riley wrenched the valve open, and a blast of scalding steam erupted from the pipes, enveloping the creature in a cloud of hissing vapor. It let out a screeching roar, thrashing wildly as the steam burned its flesh.

Elara and Ava didn't hesitate. They darted through the steam, their weapons raised. Elara drove her blade into the creature's neck, while Ava jabbed a makeshift spear into the base of its spine.

The creature let out one final, ear-splitting scream before collapsing to the ground, its massive body convulsing before going still.

For a moment, the only sound was the hiss of the steam and their own ragged breathing.

Then Kasai rushed to Milo, pulling him into a tight hug. "You did it," she whispered, her voice thick with emotion. "You're okay."

Milo grinned, though his face was pale. "Told you I could do it."

Elara wiped the blood from her blade, her eyes sharp but relieved. "We're not done yet."

Kasai nodded, her heart still racing. Mom.

They retraced their steps back to the containment unit, their footsteps echoing through the now-silent halls. When they reached the door to her mother's cell, Kasai's hands trembled as she removed the makeshift lock.

She pushed the door open, and there she was—her mother, still huddled in the corner, but alive.

Kasai rushed to her, tears streaming down her face. "I'm here, Mom. I'm here."

Her mother's arms wrapped around her, weak but warm. "I knew you'd find me," she whispered, her voice shaking with relief.

Kasai held her tightly, the fear and pain of the last few days washing over her in a wave of emotion. But they weren't done yet.

Elara's voice was soft but firm. "We need to move. More will come."

Kasai helped her mother to her feet, supporting her weight as they moved toward the exit.

They had survived The Nest.

But the fight wasn't over.

45 hours left.

Kasai's mother leaned heavily against her, each step slow and labored as they navigated the dim, sterile corridors of The Nest. The harsh fluorescent lights overhead flickered, casting long, distorted shadows along the walls. Kasai could feel her mother's frailty—every sharp bone beneath her skin, every tremor in her limbs—and it fueled a rage deep within her chest. They did this to her. The soldiers, the experiments, all of it.

But now wasn't the time for anger. Now was the time to get her out.

Elara moved ahead, her blade still slick with the blood of the mutated creature they'd just taken down. Her sharp eyes scanned every corridor, every corner, like a hawk on the hunt. Riley followed closely behind, gripping her knife tightly, her jaw clenched with tension. Milo hovered near Kasai's side, his eyes constantly darting from shadow to shadow, his baseball bat ready in his hands.

Ava brought up the rear, her face pale but determined. She knew this facility better than anyone, and her knowledge had already saved them once. But Kasai could see the fear in her eyes—the kind that came from knowing just how deep the darkness in this place ran.

They moved as quietly as possible, their footsteps muffled against the concrete floor. The hallways twisted and turned, a labyrinth of cold metal and glass. Every distant sound—a creak of the walls, the distant hum of machinery—set Kasai's nerves on edge. She kept glancing over her shoulder, half-expecting another one of those mutated creatures to burst from the shadows.

But the halls were eerily silent now. Too silent.

They reached a junction where the corridor split in two. Ava paused, glancing between the two paths.

"The left leads to the loading bay," she whispered. "It's our best shot at getting out of here without going back through the front gates. But..." She hesitated, her eyes narrowing. "They'll have guards there. Maybe more of those things."

Kasai's heart sank. Of course, it wouldn't be easy.

Elara nodded, her face grim. "Then we move fast and hit hard. We don't have time to second-guess."

Kasai adjusted her grip on her mother, feeling the woman's weight grow heavier with every step. "We'll get through this," she whispered softly, more to herself than anyone else.

They took the left corridor, moving quickly but carefully. The walls here were lined with large observation windows, giving them brief glimpses into the rooms beyond. Kasai tried not to look, but curiosity—and horror—pulled her gaze.

The rooms were filled with rows of hospital beds, each one occupied by a person strapped down, motionless. Some had IVs hooked into their arms, others were hooked to machines that beeped in slow, rhythmic patterns. But it was their faces that haunted Kasai the most. Blank. Lifeless. Eyes wide open but unseeing, as if their souls had been ripped from their bodies.

Milo whispered, his voice trembling. "What... what did they do to them?"

Ava's voice was a bitter whisper. "They're testing the serum. Trying to make them controllable. But it doesn't always work. Sometimes... sometimes it just leaves them like this."

Kasai's stomach twisted. This could've been Mom. The thought sent a fresh surge of determination through her. They had to get out of here. And they had to make sure no one else suffered this fate.

They continued down the corridor until they reached a large metal door marked Loading Bay C. Elara held up a hand, signaling for them to stop. She pressed her ear to the door, listening intently.

After a tense moment, she pulled back and whispered, "I hear at least two guards. Maybe more."

Kasai's pulse quickened. They were so close. But a wrong move here could get them all killed.

Elara turned to Ava. "Is there another way out?"

Ava shook her head. "Not from this level. We'd have to go back up, and that's riskier."

Elara cursed under her breath, then turned to Kasai and Riley. "We create a distraction. Draw the guards out, take them down, and clear a path. Milo, you stay with Kasai and her mom. Ava, you cover them from the back."

Kasai wanted to argue, to insist on helping, but she knew Elara was right. Her mom was weak—too weak to move quickly—and Kasai couldn't risk leaving her behind.

Elara and Riley slipped through the door, moving like shadows. The rest of them waited in the dim corridor, every second stretching into an eternity. Kasai's heart pounded so loudly that she was sure the guards on the other side of the door could hear it.

Then, chaos erupted.

Gunfire echoed through the loading bay, sharp and deafening in the enclosed space. Kasai flinched, tightening her grip on her mom as she tried to stay low. She could hear Elara shouting, Riley's fierce war cry, and the panicked yells of the guards as they scrambled to respond.

Milo's eyes were wide with fear, but he stood his ground, his bat raised and ready. Ava kept glancing back toward the corridor, her face tense.

Kasai knew they couldn't just sit here.

"Come on," she whispered, her voice steady despite the fear clawing at her insides. "We've got to move."

They slipped through the door, into the chaos.

The loading bay was a wide, open space filled with crates and vehicles. The flickering lights cast everything in a strobe-like haze, making it hard to tell friend from foe. Kasai spotted Elara near one of the trucks, her blade flashing as she took down a guard with swift, brutal efficiency. Riley was a blur of motion on the other side, her knife gleaming as she slashed through another attacker.

Kasai and the others moved quickly, weaving between the crates toward a large truck near the exit. Her mom was barely conscious now, her head lolling against Kasai's shoulder. But they were almost there.

Then, a gunshot rang out.

Kasai felt the air shift around her, and for a split second, she thought she'd been hit. But it wasn't her.

Milo let out a sharp cry, stumbling forward as his bat clattered to the ground. Kasai's heart stopped.

"No!" she screamed, catching him before he fell.

Blood seeped through his shirt, staining her hands as she pressed down on the wound, trying to stop the bleeding. Milo's eyes fluttered open, his face pale.

"I'm okay," he whispered, but his voice was weak.

Kasai's vision blurred with tears. "Stay with me, Milo. Please."

Elara was suddenly at their side, her face hard but her eyes filled with concern. "We've got to move, now."

Ava grabbed the keys from a fallen guard and sprinted to the truck, starting the engine with a roar. Elara lifted Milo into the back, while Kasai helped her mom into the passenger seat.

Kasai climbed in after them, cradling Milo in her arms as Elara jumped into the driver's seat. The truck roared to life, and they barreled through the loading bay doors, smashing through the gate and out into the open.

Gunfire followed them, but the trees swallowed the sound as they sped into the forest, the facility disappearing behind them.

Kasai held Milo tightly, her heart pounding in her chest. He was still breathing—but barely.

"We need to find help," she whispered, her voice shaking.

Elara nodded, her eyes locked on the road ahead. "We will. But we're not out of this yet."

Kasai looked down at Milo's pale face, her heart aching. Hold on, Milo. We're almost there.

The forest stretched out ahead of them, dark and endless.

But they were still alive.

And as long as they were breathing, there was still hope.

44 hours left.

The truck roared through the dense forest, its tires kicking up dirt and debris as it barreled down the overgrown path. The air inside was thick with tension and the metallic scent of blood. Kasai cradled Milo in her arms, his breathing shallow and uneven, his face pale and slick with sweat. Her hands were pressed tightly against the wound in his side, but no matter how much pressure she applied, the blood kept seeping through her fingers.

"Stay with me, Milo," she whispered, her voice trembling despite her best efforts to stay calm. "You're going to be okay. Just hold on."

Milo's eyelids fluttered, his lips parting in a weak attempt at a smile. "I'm... I'm okay," he whispered, but his voice was barely audible over the rumble of the truck's engine. "Just... tired."

Kasai's heart clenched. No, no, no. You're not allowed to be tired. You're going to make it. She bit her lip hard, forcing back the tears that threatened to spill. She couldn't afford to break down. Not now. Not when Milo needed her the most.

Elara gripped the steering wheel with white-knuckled hands, her eyes scanning the winding path ahead. The forest was dense, the trees closing in around them like skeletal fingers. She pushed the truck harder, weaving around fallen branches and rocks with practiced precision.

"Is there a safe place nearby?" Kasai called out, her voice hoarse from fear and exhaustion.

Ava, who was in the passenger seat, turned back, her face pale but determined. "There's an old ranger station about ten miles from here. It's abandoned, but it should have supplies. Maybe even a first aid kit."

Elara nodded, her jaw tight. "We'll make it."

Kasai wasn't sure if Elara was trying to convince her or herself, but she clung to those words like a lifeline. She looked down at Milo, brushing a strand of hair from his forehead.

"You hear that?" she whispered. "We're almost there."

Milo's eyes flickered open for a moment, and he gave her a weak nod. But Kasai could feel his body growing colder, his breathing more labored. Please, just hold on a little longer.

The truck jolted suddenly as they hit a pothole, and Milo let out a soft groan of pain. Kasai tightened her hold, murmuring soothing words even as her heart pounded with panic.

"Faster, Elara," she pleaded, her voice cracking.

"I'm going as fast as I can," Elara replied, her voice tense but steady.

The minutes stretched into an eternity as they sped through the forest. Kasai's mind raced with worst-case scenarios, each one more terrifying than the last. She couldn't lose Milo. Not after everything they'd been through. He was more than just a friend—he was family.

Finally, Ava pointed ahead. "There! The ranger station!"

Kasai's heart leapt as the small, weathered building came into view, nestled among the trees. Elara slammed on the brakes, and the truck skidded to a stop in front of the building, kicking up a cloud of dust.

Before the truck had fully stopped, Kasai was already out the door, cradling Milo in her arms as she rushed toward the station. The front door was partially open, creaking on its hinges. Elara and Riley were right behind her, weapons drawn as they scanned the area for any signs of danger.

The interior of the station was dark and dusty, but it was mercifully empty. Old maps and faded posters covered the walls, and the air smelled of mildew and wood smoke. Kasai laid Milo down on an old, dusty couch, her hands trembling as she pulled his shirt up to examine the wound.

It was worse than she'd feared. The bullet had torn through his side, and while it hadn't hit anything vital, the bleeding was severe. They needed to stop it—now.

"First aid kit!" Kasai shouted, her voice frantic. "We need a first aid kit!"

Ava was already rummaging through the cabinets, her movements frantic. After a few agonizing moments, she let out a triumphant cry and pulled out a dusty metal box with a red cross painted on the lid.

Elara grabbed the kit from her and dropped to her knees beside

Milo. "Kasai, hold him steady. Riley, get me some clean water and anything we can use as bandages."

Riley disappeared into the back room, her footsteps echoing in the silence. Kasai pressed her hands against Milo's shoulders, her heart pounding in her chest as Elara worked quickly, cleaning the wound and applying pressure to stop the bleeding.

Milo whimpered softly, his face contorted in pain. Kasai leaned down, her forehead resting against his. "You're doing great, Milo. Just a little longer, okay?"

Riley returned with a jug of water and a stack of old towels. Elara soaked one of the towels and pressed it against the wound, then pulled out a needle and thread from the kit.

"I'm going to stitch him up," Elara said, her voice calm but firm. "Kasai, keep talking to him. Keep him awake."

Kasai nodded, swallowing hard as she turned back to Milo. His eyes were half-closed, his breathing shallow. She cupped his face gently, forcing a smile onto her lips.

"Hey, remember when we found that stash of candy bars in the gas station?" she whispered, her voice soft and trembling. "You ate three of them before I even got one."

A faint smile tugged at the corners of Milo's lips. "They... were good," he mumbled, his voice barely audible.

Kasai let out a shaky laugh, tears streaming down her face. "Yeah, they were. But you still owe me one, remember?"

Milo's eyes fluttered open, and he gave her a weak nod. "I'll... I'll get you... ten."

Kasai's heart swelled with a mix of relief and heartbreak. She leaned down and kissed his forehead, her tears falling onto his skin.

"You better," she whispered, her voice breaking.

Elara worked quickly and efficiently, stitching the wound closed with practiced hands. Kasai could see the strain in Elara's eyes, the tightness in her jaw, but she didn't waver. When she was finally done, she wrapped Milo's torso in clean bandages and leaned back, letting out a long, slow breath.

"He's stable," Elara said quietly. "But he needs rest. And we need to keep an eye on him for infection."

Kasai nodded, her hands still cradling Milo's face. She could feel his pulse beneath her fingers—weak, but steady. He was alive. That was all that mattered.

Elara stood and moved to the window, peering out into the forest. Riley joined her, her knife still clutched tightly in her hand.

"We can't stay here long," Elara said, her voice low. "They'll be looking for us. We need to move as soon as Milo can travel."

Kasai didn't respond. She couldn't think about that right now. All she could focus on was Milo—his shallow breaths, the warmth of his skin beneath her hands. She wasn't going to lose him. She couldn't.

Her mother moved to sit beside her, her frail hand resting on Kasai's shoulder. "You're strong," she whispered, her voice weak but filled with pride. "Just like your father."

Kasai's heart ached at the mention of her father. She hadn't thought about him in so long—not since before everything fell apart. But hearing her mother's words gave her strength. She wasn't just fighting for herself anymore. She was fighting for Milo, for her mother, for everyone they'd lost.

"We're going to make it," Kasai whispered, more to herself than anyone else. "We have to."

The hours passed slowly, the tension in the room thick and suffocating. Kasai stayed by Milo's side, watching over him as he slept. His breathing was still shallow, but it was steady, and that gave her hope.

As night fell, the forest outside grew darker, the shadows stretching long and deep. Elara and Riley took turns keeping watch, their weapons never far from reach. Ava sat quietly in the corner, her eyes haunted by memories she didn't speak of.

Kasai finally allowed herself to close her eyes, her hand still resting on Milo's chest, feeling the steady rise and fall of his breaths. She didn't know what tomorrow would bring. She didn't know if they would make it out of this alive.

But for now, they were safe.

And as long as they were breathing, there was still hope.

30 hours left.

Chapter 9
The Gathering Storm

Kasai awoke to the faint glow of dawn filtering through the cracked windows of the ranger station. The world outside was bathed in soft, pale light, but the weight pressing down on her chest hadn't lifted. Her muscles ached, and her mind felt clouded from exhaustion, but the steady rise and fall of Milo's chest beneath her hand grounded her.

He was still alive.

That single fact was enough to pull her from the fog of sleep.

She sat up slowly, careful not to disturb him. His face was still pale, but the faint color returning to his cheeks was a small comfort. His breathing had evened out during the night, and the fever that had threatened to take him seemed to have broken. But they weren't out of danger—not yet.

Kasai glanced around the room. Elara was by the window, her sharp eyes scanning the treeline, the ever-present tension in her posture like a coiled spring. Riley sat on the floor, her back against the wall, flipping a knife between her fingers with the ease of someone who'd done it a thousand times. Ava was near the small kitchenette, sorting through what little supplies they'd scavenged from the ranger station—half a loaf of stale bread, two bottles of water, and a handful of canned beans.

Kasai's mother was still asleep on the couch opposite Milo, her breathing shallow but steady. The image of her frail body—so different from the strong, vibrant woman Kasai remembered—was a painful reminder of everything this world had taken from them.

Kasai stood quietly and crossed the room to Elara's side. The older woman didn't turn as Kasai approached, but her voice was low and steady.

"They're still out there," Elara murmured, her eyes fixed on the woods beyond. "I saw movement at dawn. Could be scouts."

Kasai's heart sank. She'd hoped the soldiers from The Nest would've lost their trail, but deep down, she knew better. People like that didn't just give up.

"How long do we have?" Kasai asked.

Elara finally turned to face her, the faint lines of exhaustion etched into her face. "Hard to say. Could be hours, could be minutes. But we need to be ready."

Kasai nodded, her jaw tightening. "Milo's still weak. He can't travel yet."

Elara's eyes softened slightly, but her voice remained firm. "I know. But if we stay here, none of us will make it."

Kasai's chest tightened. She hated the thought of moving Milo before he was ready, but the reality of their situation was undeniable. Staying here was a death sentence.

Riley's voice broke through the tension, her usual sarcasm muted by exhaustion. "Maybe we don't need to run."

Kasai turned to her, frowning. "What do you mean?"

Riley sat up, twirling the knife in her fingers. "They're hunting us because they think we're weak. What if we show them we're not?"

Kasai's stomach twisted. The idea of confronting the soldiers head-on felt like a suicide mission. But a part of her—the part that had been hardened by loss and fear—understood what Riley meant. They couldn't keep running forever.

Elara seemed to consider the idea for a moment, then shook her head. "We're outnumbered and outgunned. A direct fight isn't an option."

Ava, who had been silent until now, spoke up from the corner. "But what if we don't fight them directly?" She glanced around the room, her eyes bright with a spark of something Kasai hadn't seen before—hope. "I know the terrain around here. There are old logging roads and narrow paths through the woods. We could set traps, and create ambush points. Make them think we're everywhere."

Elara's eyes narrowed, a slow smile spreading across her face. "Guerrilla tactics."

Ava nodded. "Hit and run. Keep them off balance. If we can take out their leadership, the rest might scatter."

Kasai's heart pounded. It was risky—insanely risky—but it was better than waiting to be hunted down like animals. And if there was even a chance they could stop the soldiers from hurting anyone else...

"I'm in," Kasai said, her voice steady.

Riley grinned, the first real smile Kasai had seen from her in days. "I knew you had it in you."

Elara nodded, the decision made. "We'll split into two groups. Ava and I will set the traps. Riley, you stay with Kasai and the others. Keep them safe."

Kasai opened her mouth to protest, but Elara raised a hand to stop her.

"You've done enough, Kasai," she said gently. "You need to stay with Milo. He needs you."

Kasai swallowed the lump in her throat and nodded. She hated feeling useless, but she knew Elara was right. Milo was her priority.

As Elara and Ava gathered supplies and prepared to head out, Kasai returned to Milo's side. His eyes fluttered open as she sat down, and he gave her a weak smile.

"Are we... safe?" he whispered.

Kasai brushed his hair back from his forehead, her heart aching at how fragile he looked. "We will be," she promised.

"Elara and Ava are setting traps. We're going to stop them."

Milo's smile faded, and his eyes filled with worry. "I don't want you to get hurt."

Kasai leaned down, pressing her forehead against his. "I'm not going anywhere, Milo. I promise."

He nodded weakly, his eyes drifting closed again.

As the day wore on, Kasai, Riley, and her mother stayed inside the ranger station, listening for any signs of Elara and Ava's progress—or the soldiers. The hours dragged by, each one heavier than the last.

By late afternoon, Elara and Ava returned, their faces streaked with dirt and sweat. Elara's eyes were sharp, but there was a grim satisfaction in her expression.

"The traps are set," she announced. "They won't know what hit them."

Kasai felt a flicker of hope stir in her chest. Maybe—just maybe—they had a chance.

As night fell, the forest outside grew eerily quiet. The usual sounds of crickets and rustling leaves were replaced by a heavy, oppressive silence. Kasai sat by the window, her wrench resting in her lap, her eyes scanning the dark woods.

Then she heard it.

The faint crack of a branch snapping.

Her heart leaped into her throat.

"They're here," she whispered.

Elara moved to her side, her blade gleaming in the moonlight. "Stay calm. Stick to the plan."

The next few minutes were a blur of tension and fear. The soldiers moved through the woods with military precision, their flashlights cutting through the darkness. But they didn't expect the traps.

The first explosion rocked the forest, a deafening boom that sent birds scattering into the night sky. Kasai watched as two soldiers were thrown off their feet, their screams echoing through the trees.

Panic spread through the ranks. The soldiers fired blindly into the woods, but Elara and Ava were already moving, striking from the shadows and disappearing before anyone could react.

Kasai's heart pounded as the chaos unfolded. She wanted to help, to fight, but all she could do was wait and hope the plan worked.

Another explosion. More screams.

Then, silence.

Kasai held her breath, her eyes locked on the tree line.

Elara emerged from the shadows, her blade dripping with blood. Ava was close behind, a fierce grin on her face.

"It's over," Elara said, her voice low and steady.

Kasai felt the tension drain from her body, replaced by a wave of relief so powerful it brought tears to her eyes.

They'd done it.

They were free.

But as Kasai looked around at her friends—at Milo, pale but alive; at her mother, weak but safe; at Elara and Ava, battered but victorious—she knew this was only the beginning.

The world was still broken. The infected were still out there. But for the first time in days, Kasai felt something she hadn't dared to feel before.

Hope.

The aftermath of the ambush settled over the ranger station like a heavy fog. The distant echoes of gunfire had faded into the oppressive silence of the forest, but Kasai's heart still raced in her chest. She sat by Milo's side, her hand resting gently on his arm, feeling the faint warmth of his skin beneath her fingertips. His breathing was steady, but every rise and fall of his chest felt like a fragile miracle.

Elara moved through the room with her usual quiet intensity, checking the doors and windows, and ensuring their perimeter was secure. Ava sat at the small wooden table, her hands wrapped around a chipped mug filled with lukewarm water. Her eyes were distant, haunted by the memories of what they had just survived. Riley leaned against the wall near the door, her knife resting in her lap, fingers tapping rhythmically against the hilt. The tension in the room was palpable, a silent acknowledgment that while they had won this battle, the war was far from over.

Kasai glanced at her mother, who was propped up on a makeshift bed near the fireplace. Her face was pale, but there was a flicker of life in her eyes that hadn't been there before. She offered Kasai a weak smile, and for the first time in days, Kasai allowed herself to hope that they might actually make it out of this alive.

Elara finally broke the silence, her voice low but steady. "We can't stay here."

Kasai's stomach twisted. She knew Elara was right. The soldiers might have been scattered, but it was only a matter of time before more came looking for them. The Nest was just one piece of a larger puzzle, and Kasai could feel the weight of the unknown pressing down on her.

"Where do we go?" Riley asked, her voice sharp, cutting through the quiet like a blade.

Ava looked up from her mug, her eyes narrowing as she considered their options. "There's a safe house about twenty miles east of here," she said finally. "Old resistance outpost. It's off the grid—if we can make it there, we'll have a chance to regroup."

Elara nodded, her mind already working through the logistics. "We'll leave at first light. We can't risk traveling at night, not with Milo and your mom in this condition."

Kasai's heart clenched at the thought of moving Milo, but she knew they didn't have a choice. Staying here would be a death sentence.

"We'll make it," she whispered, more to herself than anyone else.

The hours stretched on, each minute feeling like an eternity. Kasai sat by the window, watching as the moon climbed higher into the sky, casting long shadows across the forest floor. The tension in the room never fully dissipated, but there was a sense of quiet determination among them—a fragile hope that they could survive this, that they could find a way to rebuild.

As dawn approached, Kasai felt a gentle hand on her shoulder. She turned to see Elara standing beside her, her sharp eyes softened by exhaustion and something that looked almost like pride.

"It's time," Elara said quietly.

Kasai nodded, standing and stretching her stiff limbs. She moved to Milo's side, gently shaking him awake. His eyes fluttered open, and he offered her a tired smile.

"Time to go?" he whispered, his voice hoarse but steady.

Kasai nodded, her throat tight with emotion. "Yeah. But we're going to take it slow, okay?"

Milo nodded, and with Riley's help, they managed to get him to his feet. He winced in pain but didn't complain, his determination shining through the pain. Kasai's mother was next, and though she was weak, she managed to stand with Ava's support.

They gathered what little supplies they had and stepped out into the cool morning air. The forest was eerily quiet, the usual sounds of birds and rustling leaves replaced by an oppressive silence. Kasai felt a shiver run down her spine, but she pushed it aside, focusing on the path ahead.

They moved slowly, sticking to the narrow, overgrown trails that Ava led them through. The forest closed in around them, the dense canopy blocking out most of the morning light. Every snapped twig and the rustle of leaves set Kasai's nerves on edge, but they pressed on, driven by the hope of finding safety.

Hours passed in tense silence, the only sounds of their labored breathing and the occasional grunt of pain from Milo or Kasai's mother. Kasai's muscles burned from the effort of supporting Milo's weight, but she refused to stop. Every step brought them closer to safety, closer to a future that didn't feel like it was slipping through their fingers.

As the sun climbed higher into the sky, they reached the edge of a clearing. Ava held up a hand, signaling for them to stop. She crouched low, her eyes scanning the open space ahead.

"The safe house is just beyond that ridge," she whispered, pointing to a rocky outcrop on the far side of the clearing. "But we need to be careful. This is prime ambush territory."

Elara nodded, her sharp eyes scanning the treeline. "Riley and I will go first. Make sure the path is clear."

Kasai felt her stomach twist with anxiety, but she knew Elara was right. She watched as the two women slipped into the shadows, their movements silent and precise.

The minutes stretched on, each one heavier than the last. Kasai's heart pounded in her chest, her eyes darting from shadow to shadow, expecting an attack at any moment.

Then, a single bird call echoed through the trees—a signal.

Ava let out a breath she'd been holding and nodded. "It's clear."

They moved quickly, crossing the clearing and climbing the ridge with painstaking care. Kasai's muscles screamed in protest, but she pushed through the pain, focusing on the sight of the safe house in the distance.

It was a small, unassuming cabin nestled among the trees, its weathered exterior blending seamlessly with the surrounding forest. Smoke rose faintly from the chimney, and Kasai felt a flicker of hope ignite in her chest.

They reached the cabin just as Elara and Riley emerged from the shadows, their faces grim but relieved.

"We're safe," Elara announced, her voice steady.

Kasai felt her legs give out beneath her as the tension finally broke. She sank to the ground, her arms wrapped tightly around Milo, tears streaming down her face.

They'd made it.

For the first time in what felt like forever, they were safe.

But as Kasai looked around at her friends—at the people who had become her family—she knew their journey wasn't over. The world was still broken, still dangerous. But they had each other.

And as long as they were together, they had hope.

Kasai looked up at the sky, the first rays of sunlight breaking through the trees. She felt a surge of determination rises within her.

They had survived The Nest.

Now it was time to rebuild.

35 hours left.

The cabin creaked under their weight as Kasai and the others filed inside, the door shutting behind them with a soft thud that sounded louder than it should have in the suffocating silence. The faint scent of wood smoke and damp earth clung to the air, mingling with the metallic tang of blood still lingering on their clothes. The room was dim, the only light coming from the weak rays of sunlight that filtered through cracks in the wooden shutters.

Kasai gently lowered Milo onto a worn-out mattress in the corner, his face pale and clammy, but his breathing was steady. She brushed the hair from his forehead, her heart aching at how fragile he looked. We're safe now, she reminded herself, though the tension in her chest refused to loosen.

Elara stood by the door, her sharp eyes scanning the small, single-room cabin. It was sparse—an old wooden table with mismatched chairs, a small stove in the corner, and shelves filled with dusty supplies. But it was solid. Secure. For now.

"We'll rest here," Elara said quietly, her voice carrying the weight of exhaustion. "But only for a few hours. We don't know how long it'll take for them to track us this far."

Kasai nodded, though the thought of moving again made her stomach twist. Her muscles ached, and her mind felt like it was unraveling at the edges, but she knew Elara was right. They couldn't let their guard down.

Riley slumped into one of the chairs, her knife still in hand, twirling it absentmindedly between her fingers. "Let them come," she muttered. "We'll be ready."

Ava moved to the shelves, rummaging through the supplies with quick, practiced movements. She pulled down a dusty first-aid kit and brought it over to Kasai.

"For Milo," she said softly, her eyes flicking to the boy lying unconscious on the mattress.

Kasai took the kit with a grateful nod and began tending to Milo's wound, her hands steady despite the fear gnawing at her insides. The stitches Elara had done were holding, but Milo had lost a lot of blood, and infection was a constant threat. She cleaned the wound carefully, applying fresh bandages while whispering soft reassurances to him, even though he was too weak to respond.

Her mother stirred on the other side of the room, her fragile body shivering beneath the thin blanket they'd found. Kasai's heart clenched at the sight. She wanted to be everywhere at once—helping Milo, comforting her mom, preparing for whatever came next—but the exhaustion pulled at her like gravity.

"Elara," Kasai said quietly, her voice hoarse. "What if they don't stop coming?"

Elara didn't answer immediately. She stood with her arms crossed, her eyes fixed on the dark woods beyond the window. When she finally spoke, her voice was low and steady, but there was a hint of something softer beneath the steel.

"Then we keep fighting," she said. "Until we can't anymore."

Kasai swallowed hard, nodding. She knew there was no other choice. The soldiers wouldn't stop. The Nest was just the beginning of something larger, something darker. But Kasai also knew that as long as they had each other, they had a reason to keep pushing forward.

Hours passed in a blur of whispered conversations and restless sleep. Kasai sat by Milo's side, her eyes heavy but refusing to close. Every creak of the cabin, every rustle of wind outside, made her heart jump in her chest. She couldn't shake the feeling that they were being watched—that the soldiers were out there, waiting for the perfect moment to strike.

A sudden knock at the door shattered the fragile calm.

Everyone froze.

Elara's knife was in her hand in an instant, her body tense and ready. Riley stood, her blade gleaming in the dim light. Kasai's heart pounded in her chest as she moved to shield Milo, her wrench gripped tightly in her hand.

The knock came again, softer this time.

"Who is it?" Elara called, her voice sharp and commanding.

There was a pause, then a voice—hoarse and familiar—echoed through the door.

"It's Caleb."

Kasai's heart leaped. She rushed to the door, ignoring Elara's warning glance, and yanked it open.

Caleb stood there, his face gaunt and pale, but his eyes were bright with relief. Behind him, Emma and Lucy clung to his legs, their faces smudged with dirt but otherwise unharmed.

Kasai pulled him into a tight hug, tears stinging her eyes. "I thought we lost you."

Caleb hugged her back, his voice thick with emotion. "We barely made it. But we heard the explosions. We followed the smoke."

Elara stepped forward, her eyes scanning the woods behind Caleb. "Are you sure you weren't followed?"

Caleb nodded. "We took the long way around. We're clear."

Elara hesitated for a moment, then nodded, stepping aside to let them in.

The reunion was brief, but it filled the cabin with a warmth Kasai hadn't felt in days. Emma and Lucy rushed to Milo's side, their small hands clutching his, whispering to him as if their voices alone could bring him back to consciousness.

Caleb sat at the table, his face etched with exhaustion. "We can't stay here long," he said quietly. "They're still out there. And they're not going to stop."

Ava moved to sit beside him, her voice low but firm. "There's another facility. I heard the soldiers talking about it at The Nest. It's bigger. More experiments. More prisoners."

Kasai's stomach twisted. More people suffering. More people like Mom and Milo.

"We have to stop them," she said, her voice steady despite the fear gnawing at her insides.

Elara nodded. "We will."

The decision was made before anyone could argue. They would rest for a few more hours, then move out at dawn. Their next target was the larger facility Ava had mentioned—The Hive.

Kasai sat by the fire that night, staring into the flickering flames, her mind racing with what lay ahead. They were walking into another nightmare, but this time, they knew what they were facing. They had each other. They had hope.

And for the first time in days, Kasai allowed herself to believe they might actually win.

As the fire crackled and the first light of dawn began to creep over the horizon, Kasai looked around at the faces of the people who had become her family. They were battered and broken, but they were still standing.

They were still fighting.

And as long as they were breathing, they had a chance.

27 hours left.

The first pale rays of dawn stretched through the trees, casting long, jagged shadows across the cabin floor. The fire had died down to embers, leaving only a faint warmth lingering in the room. Kasai sat with her back against the wall, staring at Milo's sleeping form, his chest rising and falling in slow, even breaths. His fever had broken overnight, but the dark circles under his eyes were a constant reminder of how close they'd come to losing him.

We're not out of this yet, Kasai thought, glancing around at the others.

Elara was awake, sitting by the window with her blade resting across her knees, her sharp eyes scanning the woods outside. She hadn't slept at all, Kasai was sure of it. Riley was sprawled on the floor, her knife tucked beneath her hand even in sleep. Ava and Caleb were whispering quietly near the table, their faces etched with exhaustion and determination. Emma and Lucy huddled together under a blanket near the fire, their small forms rising and falling in tandem.

Kasai's mother stirred on the makeshift bed in the corner, her eyes fluttering open. She looked frail, the lines on her face deeper than Kasai remembered, but there was a spark of life in her eyes that hadn't been there days ago.

"Kasai," her mother whispered, her voice hoarse but steady.

Kasai moved to her side, taking her mother's hand gently in hers. "I'm here, Mom."

Her mother's eyes filled with tears as she squeezed Kasai's hand. "You saved me."

Kasai swallowed hard, her throat tight with emotion. "We saved each other."

They sat in silence for a moment, the weight of everything they'd endured hanging heavy in the air. But there was no time to dwell on the past. The future was still uncertain, and the danger wasn't over.

Elara's voice broke the quiet, low and steady. "It's time."

Everyone stirred, the exhaustion in their eyes replaced by grim determination. They gathered their few remaining supplies—some canned food, a half-empty jug of water, and the weapons they'd scavenged from The Nest. Kasai helped Milo to his feet, his face pale but his eyes bright with stubborn resolve.

"I'm coming," he said firmly, his voice stronger than Kasai expected.

"Milo—" Kasai began, but he cut her off with a shake of his head.

"I'm not staying behind," he insisted. "We started this together. We finish it together."

Kasai nodded, her heart swelling with pride and fear. He's stronger than I ever realized.

Ava led the way out of the cabin, guiding them through the dense forest toward their next destination: The Hive. It was the facility Ava had overheard the soldiers talking about—bigger, more fortified, and the center of their experiments. If they could take it down, they might have a chance to cripple the entire operation.

The forest was eerily quiet as they moved, the only sounds were their footsteps crunching softly against the underbrush and the occasional rustle of leaves in the wind. The tension was palpable, each of them on edge, expecting an ambush at any moment.

They moved in silence, their eyes scanning the shadows, every flicker of movement setting their nerves on edge. Kasai's muscles ached from the effort of supporting Milo, but she refused to let him falter. They had come too far to give up now.

After hours of grueling travel, they reached the edge of a steep ridge overlooking a wide valley. Nestled in the center, partially hidden by the dense trees, was The Hive.

Kasai's breath caught in her throat.

The facility was massive—larger than The Nest—with high walls topped with barbed wire and guard towers at each corner.

Soldiers patrolled the perimeter in tight formations, their weapons gleaming in the midday sun. The main building loomed in the center, a cold, gray monolith of concrete and steel.

But what struck Kasai the most were the people.

Dozens of them herded like cattle through the gates, their faces pale and hollow, their eyes vacant. Some were injured, others barely able to walk, but all of them were marked with the same hopelessness Kasai had seen in her mother's eyes.

We have to stop this.

Elara crouched beside her, her eyes narrowing as she surveyed the facility. "This won't be like last time," she murmured. "They'll be expecting resistance."

Ava nodded, her face pale but resolute. "But they won't expect us."

Kasai swallowed hard, her heart pounding in her chest. "What's the plan?"

Elara traced a rough outline of the facility in the dirt with her knife. "We'll split into two groups. Ava and I will create a diversion at the front gate, to draw their attention. Kasai, you, and Riley will take Milo and the others through the service tunnels Ava mentioned. They'll be less guarded, but you'll need to move fast."

Kasai's stomach twisted at the thought of separating again, but she nodded. They had no other choice.

Riley grinned, twirling her knife in her hand. "Sounds like fun."

Kasai forced a smile, though her heart felt heavy. She turned to Milo, her eyes searching his face for any sign of hesitation.

"Are you sure you're up for this?" she asked quietly.

Milo nodded, his jaw set with determination. "I'm sure."

Kasai squeezed his hand, drawing strength from his resolve. They had faced impossible odds before. They could do it again.

As the sun began to dip below the horizon, they moved into position. The forest grew darker, the shadows deepening as they approached The Hive.

Elara and Ava slipped away toward the front gate, their figures disappearing into the growing gloom. Kasai led the others toward the service tunnels, her heart pounding with every step.

The entrance was hidden behind a cluster of rocks near the edge of the facility. Ava had given them detailed instructions on how to find it, but Kasai's hands still trembled as she pried the rusted hatch open.

The tunnel beyond was dark and narrow, the air thick with the stench of mildew and decay. Kasai led the way, her flashlight cutting through the gloom, Riley close behind with Milo and the others following in tense silence.

The walls felt like they were closing in around her, each step echoing in the confined space. But Kasai kept moving, her mind focused on the goal ahead.

They reached a junction where the tunnel split in two. Kasai hesitated, trying to remember Ava's directions.

"Left," Milo whispered, his voice steady despite the pain etched into his features.

Kasai nodded, trusting him without hesitation. They turned left, moving deeper into the tunnel.

The sound of gunfire erupted above them, sharp and deafening in the confined space. Kasai's heart leaped into her throat. Elara and Ava have started the diversion.

"We need to move," Riley hissed, her eyes flashing in the dim light.

They picked up the pace, their footsteps quickening as they navigated the twisting tunnels. The sound of gunfire grew louder, mingling with the distant shouts of soldiers.

Finally, they reached a metal grate at the end of the tunnel. Kasai peered through the slats, her heart pounding in her chest.

They were directly beneath the main building.

Kasai turned to the others, her eyes blazing with determination. "This is it."

Riley nodded, her grip tightening on her knife. "Let's finish this."

Kasai pried the grate open, the metal groaning in protest. She climbed through, her heart pounding with fear and adrenaline.

The facility was larger up close, the cold, sterile hallways stretching out before them like a maze. But Kasai didn't hesitate.

She led the way, her mind focused on finding the prisoners—and stopping whatever horrors were happening inside.

They moved through the halls like shadows, avoiding patrols and slipping past locked doors. The facility was a labyrinth, but Kasai's determination kept them moving.

Finally, they reached a large, reinforced door marked Containment. Kasai's stomach twisted as she stared at it, knowing what lay beyond.

She turned to the others, her voice low but steady. "This is it."

Riley nodded, her eyes sharp. "Let's end this."

Kasai pushed the door open, her heart pounding in her chest.

And what she saw on the other side made her blood run cold.

Rows of people were strapped to metal tables, their eyes wide and unseeing, their bodies convulsing as strange, glowing liquid was pumped into their veins. The air was thick with the stench of chemicals and something far worse—death.

Kasai's stomach lurched, but she forced herself to move.

"We have to stop this," she whispered, her voice trembling with rage.

Riley nodded, her face pale but resolute. "We will."

They moved through the room, freeing the prisoners and disabling the machines. The soldiers guarding the room were caught off guard, and Riley took them down with brutal efficiency.

Kasai reached the last table, her heart pounding as she recognized the face of the person strapped down.

It was Daniel.

His eyes flickered open, a twisted grin spreading across his face.

"You can't stop it," he whispered, his voice a hoarse rasp. "It's already begun."

Kasai's blood ran cold.

But she didn't hesitate.

She raised her wrench and brought it down with all her strength, silencing him once and for all.

As the echoes of the final blow faded into the silence, Kasai stood over his lifeless body, her chest heaving with exhaustion and rage.

They had stopped The Hive.

But the war wasn't over.

And as long as they were breathing, they would keep fighting.

28 hours left.

Kasai stood over Daniel's lifeless body, her wrench slick with blood, her breath coming in ragged gasps. The room around her was a symphony of chaos—alarms blaring, the harsh flicker of red emergency lights casting everything in a nightmarish glow. But all Kasai could focus on was the finality of this moment. Daniel, the man who had hunted them, tortured her friends and turned The Nest into a nightmare, was finally gone.

But his last words echoed in her mind.

"It's already begun."

Kasai's heart pounded as the weight of those words settled over her. Whatever Daniel had meant, it wasn't just about The Hive. There was something bigger at play—something they hadn't stopped.

"Elara, we need to move!" Riley's voice snapped Kasai out of her thoughts. She turned to see Riley helping a dazed prisoner off one of the metal tables, while Milo leaned heavily against the wall, his face pale but his eyes sharp.

Kasai nodded, wiping the sweat from her brow. "Let's get everyone out."

They moved quickly, freeing the remaining prisoners and guiding them toward the service tunnels. The facility was in disarray, the soldiers thrown into confusion by the alarms and the unexpected resistance. But Kasai knew it wouldn't take long for them to regroup.

As they navigated the narrow, dimly lit tunnels, Kasai felt the hours slipping away. The adrenaline coursing through her veins blurred time, turning minutes into what felt like seconds. She could feel the urgency in every step, the knowledge that they were running out of time—not just to escape, but to stop whatever Daniel had hinted at.

By the time they emerged from the tunnels and into the dense forest beyond The Hive, the sun was already high in the sky.

Kasai's muscles burned with exhaustion, but she pushed forward, her mind racing with possibilities. What had Daniel meant? What else were the soldiers planning?

They didn't stop moving until they reached the relative safety of an abandoned farmhouse several miles from The Hive. The building was dilapidated, with broken windows and a sagging roof, but it was shelter. For now, it was enough.

Kasai collapsed onto the wooden floor, her chest heaving as she tried to catch her breath. Milo sat beside her, his face drawn with exhaustion, but there was a spark of determination in his eyes that gave Kasai strength.

Elara moved through the room, checking the windows and securing the doors, while Riley tended to the injured prisoners. Ava sat at the kitchen table, a map spread out before her, her brow furrowed in concentration.

Kasai's mother sat quietly in the corner, her eyes closed, but her breathing steady. The sight of her alive and safe filled Kasai with a warmth that cut through the exhaustion, but it was fleeting. They weren't done yet.

"Elara," Kasai called, her voice hoarse. "What did Daniel mean? What's already begun?"

Elara paused, her eyes narrowing as she considered the question. "I don't know," she admitted. "But whatever it is, it's bigger than The Hive."

Ava looked up from the map, her face pale. "I heard them talking," she said quietly. "Before we escaped The Nest. They mentioned something called The Core. It's a central hub for all their operations. If Daniel was right... that's where it's happening."

Kasai's heart sank. The Core. It sounded like the heart of everything—the experiments, the soldiers, the infection. If they didn't stop it, nothing they'd done would matter.

"We have to find it," Kasai said firmly.

Elara nodded, her expression grim. "We will. But we need to move fast."

They spent the next few hours gathering supplies and tending to the wounded. Kasai felt the time slipping through her fingers, each tick of the clock a reminder that they were racing against an enemy they barely understood.

By nightfall, they were on the move again, navigating through the dense forest under the cover of darkness. The moon cast an eerie glow over the trees, their shadows stretching long and thin across the ground. Kasai could feel the exhaustion in every step, but she pushed forward, driven by the knowledge that they were close—so close—to ending this.

They reached the outskirts of The Core just before dawn. The facility was even more imposing than The Hive—a sprawling complex of steel and concrete, surrounded by high walls and guarded by soldiers armed to the teeth. But it was what lay beyond the walls that made Kasai's blood run cold.

Dozens of infected—mutated, grotesque versions of what they had seen before—were corralled in large, electrified pens. Their eyes glowed faintly in the dim light, and their movements were erratic as if they were being controlled.

"They're building an army," Riley whispered, her voice filled with horror.

Kasai felt her stomach twist. This is what Daniel meant. They weren't just experimenting on people—they were turning them into weapons.

"We have to stop this," Kasai said, her voice steady despite the fear clawing at her insides.

Elara nodded, her eyes sharp. "We hit them hard and fast. Take out the generators, and disable their control systems. We can't let them unleash those things."

Kasai turned to Milo, her heart aching at the sight of him so pale and weak, but his eyes were filled with the same fierce determination she felt burning in her chest.

"You stay here," she said quietly. "Keep the others safe."

Milo opened his mouth to argue, but Kasai shook her head. "I need you to do this, Milo. You're the strongest person I know. I need to know someone's watching their backs."

Milo hesitated, then nodded, his jaw set. "Be careful."

Kasai squeezed his hand, then turned to join Elara and Riley. Together, they slipped through the shadows, moving toward The

Core with a singular purpose: to end this once and for all.

The hours that followed were a blur of chaos and violence. They moved through the facility like ghosts, disabling systems, freeing prisoners, and taking down guards with ruthless efficiency. The infected broke free from their pens, turning on their captors in a wave of uncontrollable fury.

Kasai felt the weight of every decision, every life they saved—and everyone they couldn't. But there was no time to grieve. Not yet.

As they reached the central control room, Kasai's heart pounded in her chest. The room was filled with monitors displaying live feeds of other facilities—there were more. But if they could shut down The Core, they could cripple the entire operation.

Elara moved to the control panel, her fingers flying over the keys. "This is it," she said, her voice low but steady.

Kasai felt a surge of determination as she moved to help, but before they could finish, the door burst open.

A group of soldiers stormed in, their rifles raised.

But Kasai didn't hesitate.

She swung her wrench with all the strength she had left, the weight of every loss, every fear, and every hope driving her forward.

The fight was brutal, but they emerged victorious, their bodies battered but unbroken.

Elara finished the shutdown sequence, and as the facility's lights flickered and died, Kasai felt a wave of relief wash over her.

It was over.

They had won.

As they emerged into the dawn light, the first rays of the sun casting the world in a soft, golden glow, Kasai felt something she hadn't dared to feel in days.

Hope.

They had survived.

And as long as they were breathing, they would rebuild.

24 hours left.

Chapter 10
A New Dawn

The world felt unnerving still as Kasai stepped out of The Core, the cold morning air biting against her sweat-soaked skin. The rising sun bathed the horizon in a warm, golden glow, but it did little to chase away the exhaustion gnawing at her bones. For the first time in what felt like forever, the deafening sounds of chaos—the gunfire, the inhuman screams of the infected, the frantic shouts of soldiers—had faded into silence.

Kasai stood at the edge of the facility, staring out at the forest that had become both a sanctuary and a battleground. Her chest rose and fell with heavy breaths, each inhale reminding her she was still alive, still standing. But survival came with its own weight, a heavy burden that pressed down on her shoulders.

It's over, she thought, but the words felt hollow.

Elara appeared beside her, her face smeared with dirt and blood, but her eyes sharp and alert. The lines of exhaustion etched into her skin made her look older, but there was a flicker of something else there too—relief.

"We did it," Elara said quietly, her voice hoarse from shouting and the strain of the night. She glanced at Kasai, a rare softness in her gaze. "You did it."

Kasai shook her head, the weight of their losses pressing against her chest. "We did it. But... it doesn't feel over."

Elara nodded, understanding flickering in her eyes. "Because it's not. Not really."

Kasai turned to look back at The Core, the once-imposing structure now dark and lifeless. Smoke curled from the shattered windows, and the ground was littered with the remnants of their battle—broken weapons, crumpled bodies, and bloodstains that would never wash away. The infected that had been released roamed aimlessly beyond the facility's walls, their monstrous forms retreating into the woods now that the soldiers' control systems had been destroyed.

Riley stumbled out of the facility a few moments later, her knife still gripped tightly in her hand. She was limping, a fresh gash on her leg, but the defiant grin on her face remained intact.

"Damn," Riley muttered, wiping sweat from her brow. "I was hoping for at least one more fight."

Kasai managed a weak smile, the tension in her chest easing slightly. Riley's irreverent humor had been one of the few things that kept them grounded through the worst of it.

Ava emerged next, her arm slung around Caleb's shoulders for support. The man's face was pale, and his movements were stiff, but there was a spark in his eyes that hadn't been there before— a spark of hope. Emma and Lucy trailed behind them, their small faces streaked with dirt but their eyes wide with wonder.

Kasai's heart clenched when she saw Milo being carried by two of the freed prisoners, his face pale but peaceful. She rushed forward, her knees nearly giving out as she dropped beside him.

"Milo," she whispered, brushing his sweat-dampened hair from his forehead. His eyes fluttered open, and for a moment, Kasai was afraid he wouldn't recognize her. But then his lips curled into a faint smile.

"Told you... I'd get you that candy bar," he rasped weakly.

Kasai let out a shaky laugh, tears streaming down her cheeks. "You better. I'm holding you to that."

Milo's smile faded slightly, his eyes clouding with something deeper—pain, maybe, or the weight of everything they'd lost. "Is it over?"

Kasai swallowed hard, glancing back at The Core, the dark, broken heart of everything they had fought against. She thought of Daniel's words, of the other facilities they had seen on the monitors. It's already begun.

"No," Kasai whispered, her voice steady despite the lump in her throat. "But we stopped this. And that's a start."

They stayed there for a while, basking in the fragile silence that followed their victory. The sky above them brightened, the sun climbing higher, casting long shadows across the battlefield. The forest seemed to hold its breath as if the world itself was waiting to see what they would do next.

Elara was the first to move, her voice cutting through the quiet. "We can't stay here."

Kasai nodded, wiping the tears from her cheeks. "Where do we go?"

Ava stepped forward, her eyes scanning the horizon. "There are still people out there—other survivors, other facilities. We need to find them. Help them."

Kasai felt a surge of determination rises within her, pushing back the exhaustion that threatened to drag her down. She looked around at the faces of the people who had become her family—Elara, Riley, Ava, Caleb, Milo, her mother, and the kids. They had survived the impossible. They had faced monsters—human and otherwise—and come out the other side.

They weren't just survivors.

They were fighters.

Kasai stood, her muscles protesting, but her resolve unwavering. "Then we find them. We fight. We make sure this doesn't happen again."

Elara placed a hand on Kasai's shoulder, her grip firm but warm. "You've come a long way, Kasai."

Kasai met her gaze, a fierce light burning in her eyes. "And we've got a long way to go."

They gathered their supplies, helped the injured and the weak, and began the long trek away from The Core. The forest swallowed them up, the towering trees standing as silent sentinels to their journey. The road ahead was uncertain, filled with dangers they couldn't yet imagine, but Kasai felt a strange sense of peace settles over her.

They were no longer running.

They were moving forward.

Hours bled into one another as they traveled, the landscape shifting from dense forests to open fields, and eventually to the outskirts of a shattered town. Buildings stood like hollowed-out skeletons, their windows shattered, their walls scorched from fires long extinguished. But there were signs of life—small, fragile signs. A curtain fluttering in a broken window, the faint sound of laughter drifting from a hidden alleyway, the distant flicker of a fire in the twilight.

They weren't alone.

As night fell, they made camp in an old library, the walls lined with dusty books that smelled of ink and time. Kasai sat by the fire, Milo resting against her shoulder, his breathing steady and warm. Her mother sat across from them, her eyes reflecting the dancing flames, a faint smile playing on her lips.

Riley sharpened her knife nearby, her expression uncharacteristically thoughtful. "You think we'll ever get back to normal?" she asked, her voice cutting through the quiet.

Kasai stared into the fire, considering the question. Normal. It felt like a foreign concept, something from another lifetime. But maybe normal wasn't what they needed.

"Maybe not," Kasai said finally. "But we'll build something better."

Riley snorted softly, but there was no bite in her tone. "Better, huh? That's a tall order."

Kasai smiled a small, genuine smile that felt strange on her face after everything they'd been through. "We've faced worse."

They sat in comfortable silence for a while, the crackle of the fire the only sound. Kasai's mind wandered, thinking of the road ahead—the people they would meet, the battles they would fight, the world they would rebuild.

And for the first time in days, weeks, maybe even months, she felt hope.

Real, unshakable hope.

As she drifted off to sleep, Milo's head resting against her shoulder and the warmth of her family surrounding her, Kasai knew one thing for certain.

They had survived 72 hours.

Now, it was time to live.

0 hours left.

\Kasai awoke to the faint glow of morning light streaming through the broken windows of the old library. The soft rustling of pages and the quiet breathing of her friends created a fragile sense of peace, a calm she hadn't felt in what seemed like forever. For a moment, she let herself believe they were safe, that the world outside had somehow healed overnight.

But the reality was never that kind.

She shifted slightly, careful not to wake Milo, whose head was still resting against her shoulder. His breathing was steady, but she could feel the lingering fragility in his body. The fever had broken, and the color had returned to his cheeks, but Kasai knew the road to recovery would be long.

Across the room, her mother stirred, her thin frame wrapped in a worn blanket they'd scavenged from the library. Despite the lines of exhaustion etched into her face, there was a softness in her expression that Kasai hadn't seen since before the outbreak. It gave Kasai hope—a fragile, flickering thing, but hope nonetheless.

Elara was already awake, of course. She sat by the window, her sharp eyes scanning the deserted streets beyond. Her knife rested on her knee, and her posture was tense, but there was a sense of quiet satisfaction in the set of her jaw. They'd won a battle. Maybe not the war, but a battle.

Riley lay sprawled on a pile of old books, her arm flung over her eyes to block out the light. Even in sleep, her hand was never far from her knife. Ava was curled up near the fire, a map spread out beside her, her face peaceful for the first time since they'd left The Core. Caleb sat nearby, his arm around Emma and Lucy, who were still fast asleep, their small faces relaxed in a way that made

Kasai's heartache.

They deserved this peace. They all did.

But deep down, Kasai knew it wouldn't last.

She gently shifted Milo off her shoulder, grabbing her wrench and standing up with a quiet groan. Her body ached from days of non-stop fighting, but the weight of exhaustion was something she'd grown used to. She moved to the window beside Elara, staring out at the ruined town beyond.

The streets were eerily quiet, the remnants of a world long gone scattered across cracked pavement and crumbling buildings. Rusted cars sat abandoned in the middle of the road, their windows shattered and their tires flat. Faded signs hung from storefronts, advertising businesses that no longer existed. But there were signs of life, too—faint trails of smoke rising in the distance, the occasional flicker of movement in the shadows.

"There's still people out there," Kasai murmured, her breath fogging up the dirty glass.

Elara nodded, her eyes never leaving the horizon. "Yeah. And they'll need our help."

Kasai swallowed hard, her mind racing with thoughts of what came next. They'd survived The Core, but that didn't mean the fight was over. The soldiers might have been scattered, but their experiments—the infection—were still out there. And Daniel's final words echoed in her mind like a haunting refrain.

It's already begun.

Kasai turned to Elara, her voice quiet but firm. "We can't stay here. We need to find the others—the survivors. We need to stop whatever else is out there."

Elara's lips pressed into a thin line, but she didn't argue. She simply nodded, her eyes filled with the same determination Kasai felt burning in her chest. "We'll leave after breakfast. Let everyone rest a bit longer."

Kasai nodded, but her mind was already moving ahead, planning their next steps. She moved back to the fire, where Ava was beginning to stir. The older girl blinked blearily, rubbing the sleep from her eyes.

"We need to move soon," Kasai said softly, sitting down beside her. "But I wanted to talk to you first."

Ava's eyes sharpened instantly, all traces of sleep vanishing as she sat up straighter. "What's on your mind?"

Kasai hesitated for a moment, then gestured toward the map Ava had been studying. "You heard them talking at The Nest. You know more about their plans than the rest of us. Do you think there are more places like The Core?"

Ava's face darkened, her fingers tracing the lines on the map. "I'm sure of it. The Core wasn't just a facility—it was a hub. A nerve center. But it wasn't the only one." She pointed to a spot on the map, a small town miles away from where they were now. "I overheard one of the soldiers mention this place. Said it was the next phase of their project."

Kasai felt a chill run down her spine. Next phase.

"We need to stop it," she said quietly. "Before they hurt more people."

Ava nodded, folding the map carefully and tucking it into her pack. "We will."

By the time the sun had fully risen, everyone was awake, and the library was filled with quiet chatter as they prepared to move. Riley handed out the last of their food—canned beans and stale crackers—and Caleb helped Emma and Lucy pack up their few belongings.

Kasai moved to Milo's side, crouching down to meet his tired gaze. "You up for this?" she asked gently, her hand resting on his shoulder.

Milo gave her a weak but determined smile. "I'll keep up. I promise."

Kasai ruffled his hair, her heart swelling with pride. He'd been through more than any kid should, but he was still standing. They all were.

As they stepped out of the library and into the bright morning light, Kasai felt a surge of determination rise within her. The world was broken, but they weren't. They had survived the impossible and faced horrors that would haunt them forever. But they were still here.

Still fighting.

They moved through the town in silence, their footsteps echoing off the crumbling walls. The air was thick with the scent of smoke and decay, but there was something else too—hope. It clung to them like a second skin, fragile but unyielding.

As they reached the outskirts of the town, Kasai glanced back at the people who had become her family. Elara, with her fierce determination. Riley, with her sharp wit and unwavering loyalty. Ava, with her quiet strength. Caleb, with his gentle heart. Milo, her little brother in everything but blood. Her mother was alive and safe. Emma and Lucy, are innocent and full of potential.

They were more than survivors.

They were a new beginning.

Kasai turned to face the road ahead, the sun casting long shadows across the cracked pavement. The journey wouldn't be easy. The battles ahead would test them in ways they couldn't yet imagine. But they were ready.

They had survived 72 hours in a world that had tried to break them.

Now, it was time to rebuild.

Kasai tightened her grip on her wrench, the weight of it familiar and comforting in her hand. She took a deep breath, the cool morning air filling her lungs, and stepped forward.

The road stretched out before them, long and uncertain.

But they weren't afraid.

Because they had each other.

And as long as they were breathing, there was hope.

Always hope.

The sun climbed higher as Kasai and her group followed the cracked road out of the ruined town, each step echoing against the silence of a world that had changed beyond recognition. The once-thriving landscape was now a graveyard of civilization, with rusted cars overtaken by weeds and buildings crumbling under the weight of abandonment. But Kasai didn't see just the ruins. She saw possibilities. A chance to rebuild.

Milo walked beside her, his steps slower than usual, but his resolve as fierce as ever. Every time his foot faltered, Kasai would steady him with a hand on his shoulder, and he'd flash her a quick, determined smile. She knew he was pushing himself harder than he should, but there was no arguing with Milo when he had that look in his eyes. He wanted to feel useful, to be a part of whatever came next.

Ahead, Elara led the way, her blade strapped to her side, her gaze scanning the horizon for danger. She was silent, as always, but there was a different energy in the way she moved—less the tension of someone constantly preparing for an ambush and more the purpose of a leader guiding her people toward something better. Kasai admired her strength, even when Elara refused to acknowledge it herself.

Riley, on the other hand, hadn't lost her edge. She sauntered a few paces behind, her knife spinning between her fingers as if daring the universe to throw another challenge their way. Kasai caught her murmuring to herself more than once, little snippets of sarcasm about the state of the world, but beneath the bravado, Kasai knew Riley cared deeply. She'd risked her life for all of them more times than Kasai could count.

Ava and Caleb followed closely, with Emma and Lucy between them. The girls skipped along, oblivious to the weight of the world, their laughter light and sweet like the wind rustling through the trees. Seeing them so carefree, even after everything, made Kasai's heart ache with both sadness and hope. If they could still find joy in this broken world, maybe there was a chance for everyone else.

Kasai's mother walked beside Caleb, her face drawn but peaceful. Every so often, she would glance at Kasai, and their eyes would meet in a silent exchange of gratitude and love. Kasai hadn't dared hope for this reunion when the world had fallen apart. And now that they were together again, she wasn't letting go.

They traveled for hours, the heat of the day bearing down on them, sweat dripping down their backs as they pushed forward. The road was long, but no one complained. They were all too focused on the goal ahead—finding the other survivors and dismantling whatever remnants of The Core still lingered in the shadows.

By midday, they reached a small rise overlooking a valley. From their vantage point, Kasai could see a cluster of makeshift buildings nestled among the trees. Smoke curled lazily from chimneys and the faint sound of voices carried on the wind.

"A settlement," Elara murmured, lowering her binoculars. "Looks like they've fortified it pretty well."

Kasai felt a flicker of hope ignite in her chest. More survivors. People who had weathered the storm just like they had. But with that hope came caution. Not everyone they'd met since the world fell apart had been kind. Trust was a rare commodity these days.

"Think they'll let us in?" Riley asked, twirling her knife before sliding it back into her belt.

Elara didn't answer immediately. She studied the settlement for a long moment before finally nodding. "We'll approach carefully. No sudden moves."

Kasai adjusted her grip on her wrench, her heart pounding with a mix of anticipation and nerves. She exchanged a glance with Milo, who gave her a small, reassuring nod. Whatever happens, we face it together.

They descended the hill, their movements slow and deliberate. As they approached the settlement, Kasai noticed the barricades made from scrap metal and wood, reinforced with what looked like car parts and pieces of old fences. It was clear these people knew how to defend themselves.

A figure emerged from behind one of the barricades, a rifle slung over his shoulder. He was tall and broad-shouldered, with a weathered face that spoke of years of hardship. His eyes narrowed as he spotted them, but he didn't raise his weapon.

"Travelers?" he called out, his voice gruff but not unkind.

Elara stepped forward, her hands raised slightly to show she meant no harm. "We're survivors. Looking for shelter—and information."

The man studied them for a moment longer before nodding. He gestured for them to approach. "You'll find both here, but don't try anything. We've had enough trouble from strangers."

Kasai felt the tension ease slightly as they were led into the settlement. The people inside were wary but curious, their eyes following the newcomers as they passed. The settlement was small but organized, with gardens growing in neat rows and children playing near a makeshift schoolhouse.

They were led to the center of the settlement, where a woman with silver-streaked hair and piercing green eyes waited. She wore a patchwork jacket, and her hands were calloused from years of hard work.

"I'm Nora," she introduced herself, her gaze sweeping over the group. "Leader of this settlement. You look like you've been through hell."

Kasai nodded. "We have. But we're still standing."

Nora's lips curled into a faint smile. "That's more than most can say these days. Come, sit. Tell me your story."

They gathered around a large fire pit, and Kasai recounted everything—The Nest, The Hive, and The Core. She spoke of Daniel, the soldiers, and the experiments they'd uncovered. As she spoke, she noticed the expressions of the people around them shift from curiosity to horror, and finally to anger.

When she finished, Nora was silent for a long moment, her eyes dark with thought. Finally, she spoke. "We've heard rumors of places like The Core, but no one's ever survived to tell the tale. You've done more than just survive—you've struck a blow against them."

Elara leaned forward, her voice low. "But it's not over. We need to find the other facilities. We need to stop this for good."

Nora nodded, her eyes gleaming with determination. "Then you're not alone. We've been gathering people from all over. Fighters, survivors. We've been waiting for a chance to strike back."

A ripple of hope passed through Kasai. They weren't alone. There were others out there, just like them, ready to fight for a better future.

As the sun began to set, casting the settlement in warm, golden light, Kasai felt a sense of peace settle over her. For the first time in a long while, the future didn't feel like a dark, looming shadow. It felt like a blank canvas, waiting for them to paint a new story.

Later that night, as the stars stretched across the sky in a glittering tapestry, Kasai sat by the fire with Milo, Elara, and the others. The flames danced in their eyes, reflecting the quiet determination that burned within each of them.

"What now?" Milo asked softly, his voice steady despite the exhaustion in his eyes.

Kasai stared into the fire for a long moment before answering. "Now, we rebuild. We find the others. We finish what we started."

Milo nodded, a small smile tugging at the corners of his lips. "Together?"

Kasai reached out, ruffling his hair affectionately. "Always."

As the night stretched on, Kasai felt the weight of the past few days lifting, replaced by something stronger—hope. They had survived 72 hours in a world that had tried to break them, but now, they were more than survivors.

They were a family.

And as long as they were together, they could face anything the world threw at them.

The road ahead would be long and difficult, filled with battles yet to come. But Kasai knew one thing for certain.

They had each other.

And that was enough.

The night air in the settlement was cooler than Kasai had expected. It wrapped around her like a blanket, bringing with it the scent of wood smoke and damp earth. She sat by the fire, staring into the flickering flames as the sounds of the camp settled into a soft, rhythmic hum—low conversations, the occasional crack of firewood, and the quiet rustling of people finding comfort in the safety they hadn't known for far too long.

It felt strange to be still, to not be running or fighting. Kasai's muscles ached with the unfamiliarity of rest. But beneath that, a deeper ache throbbed—a grief she hadn't let herself feel until now.

She thought of everyone they'd lost along the way. The friends whose faces were now just memories, the families torn apart by the infection, the strangers they couldn't save. Even with the victory at The Core, it felt like too little, too late.

Beside her, Milo stirred, his head resting on her shoulder. His breathing was slow and steady, the color finally returning to his face after days of battling his injuries. Kasai wrapped an arm around him, holding him close as if by sheer will she could keep him safe from everything the world might throw at them next.

"I thought we'd never get here," Milo whispered, his voice rough with exhaustion but filled with something Kasai hadn't heard in his voice for days—hope.

Kasai smiled softly, though it didn't quite reach her eyes. "Me too."

Milo lifted his head to look at her, his eyes shining in the firelight. "But we did. We made it."

Kasai nodded, swallowing the lump rising in her throat. They had made it, but the journey wasn't over. Not yet.

Across the fire, Elara sat sharpening her blade, her eyes flickering up every now and then to scan the camp. She was never fully at ease, even now, surrounded by allies and walls. But there was a looseness in her posture that hadn't been there before—a sign that even the most hardened among them felt the weight of their survival lifting.

Riley lounged nearby, her boots propped up on a log, idly tossing her knife into the air and catching it with a lazy precision that belied the sharpness of her mind. She was watching Kasai, a smirk tugging at the corner of her mouth.

"You're thinking too hard, Kasai," Riley teased her voice light but edged with sincerity. "It's okay to breathe, you know."

Kasai chuckled softly, shaking her head. "I think I forgot how."

Riley's grin softened. "We all did."

Ava approached the fire with Caleb and the girls trailing behind her. She held a worn map in her hands, the edges frayed from constant folding and unfolding. She spread it out on the ground between them, the flickering light casting shadows over the lines and markings.

"I've been thinking," Ava said, her voice low but steady. "About what's next."

Kasai leaned forward, her heart picking up speed. What's next had been the question haunting her since they left The Core. They'd stopped one facility, but the infection wasn't gone. The soldiers weren't gone. The world wasn't fixed.

Ava pointed to a cluster of markings on the map. "I overheard the soldiers at The Core talking about other sites—places where they were setting up new experiments, new control systems. The Core was just the beginning."

Kasai's stomach twisted. She'd known it deep down, but hearing it confirmed sent a fresh wave of determination through her.

"How many?" Elara asked her voice like steel.

Ava hesitated, then shook her head. "I don't know. But enough to matter."

Silence fell over the group as the weight of Ava's words sank in. They'd fought so hard to take down The Core, but the battle wasn't over. It might never be over.

Kasai felt Milo's hand slip into hers, his grip surprisingly strong. She squeezed back, drawing strength from the simple connection.

"We can't stop now," Kasai said finally, her voice steady despite the fear curling in her chest. "If there are more places like The Core, we need to find them. We need to stop them."

Elara nodded, sliding her blade back into its sheath. "We'll need supplies. Weapons. People."

Nora, the leader of the settlement, stepped into the firelight then, her face shadowed but her eyes bright with determination. She'd been listening from the edges, letting them plan, but now she spoke.

"You'll have our support," Nora said firmly. "We've been waiting for people like you—fighters, leaders. We've been surviving, but it's time we start fighting back."

Kasai felt a surge of gratitude toward Nora and the people of the settlement. They weren't just survivors—they were ready to reclaim their world.

Riley stretched, cracking her knuckles with a grin. "Well, looks like we've got ourselves a revolution."

The fire crackled, casting sparks into the night sky. Kasai

stared into the flames, imagining the battles ahead—the dangers, the losses, the impossible choices. But she also saw something else: a future. One they could build together.

As the night stretched on, plans began to form. Maps were marked, routes were discussed, and alliances were forged. The camp buzzed with a new energy, a collective purpose that bound them all together.

But Kasai couldn't shake the feeling that time was slipping through their fingers.

Later, when the fire had burned low and most of the camp had drifted off to sleep, Kasai found herself standing at the edge of the settlement, staring out into the dark forest. The stars above were brilliant, unmarred by city lights, and for a moment, she let herself believe the world could be beautiful again.

Elara approached quietly, her presence a steady, grounding force. She didn't say anything at first, just stood beside Kasai, staring out into the night.

"You did good," Elara said finally, her voice softer than Kasai had ever heard it.

Kasai shook her head, her throat tight. "We all did."

Elara nodded, then turned to face her fully. "But you led us. You kept us together."

Kasai felt the weight of those words settle over her, heavier than any weapon she'd ever carried. She'd never seen herself as a leader. She was just trying to survive, just trying to protect the people she loved.

But maybe that was enough.

"I'm scared," Kasai admitted quietly, her voice barely above a whisper.

Elara placed a firm hand on her shoulder. "Good. It means you care. But don't let it stop you."

Kasai nodded, drawing in a deep breath. She wouldn't let it stop her. She couldn't.

As dawn broke over the horizon, casting the world in a soft, golden light, Kasai returned to the camp. She looked at the faces of the people who had become her family—Milo, her mother, Elara, Riley, Ava, Caleb, Emma, and Lucy. They had survived the impossible. They had faced monsters and come out the other side.

And now, they were ready to rebuild.

Kasai picked up her wrench, the weight of it familiar and comforting in her hand. She felt the tension in the camp shift as others began to stir, their eyes meeting hers with the same determination burning in their chests.

They were ready.

Kasai turned to face the road ahead, the sun rising behind her, casting long shadows that stretched out before them.

"Let's finish this," she said, her voice strong and unwavering.

And together, they stepped into the new dawn, ready to fight for a future they could finally believe in.

The sun climbed higher in the sky as Kasai led the group down the winding road, the golden light filtering through the trees, casting dappled shadows across the cracked pavement. The world felt different now—still broken, still dangerous, but no longer suffocating under the weight of fear. For the first time since the outbreak, there was a sense of direction, of purpose. They weren't just running anymore.

They were fighting for something.

Kasai glanced over her shoulder at the people walking beside her, each one a symbol of survival. Milo, his steps slower but steady, kept pace with a quiet determination that made Kasai's heart swell with pride. He'd faced death and come out stronger, and she knew that whatever lay ahead, he would be ready.

Her mother walked just behind them, her fragile frame supported by Caleb's steady arm. Despite the toll the infection had taken on her body, there was a spark in her eyes that Kasai hadn't seen in years—a light that spoke of hope and resilience. She'd fought her way back from the brink, and now she was here, part of something bigger.

Elara was at the front of the group, her sharp eyes scanning the horizon for any signs of danger. She moved with the same precision and focus that had kept them alive through countless battles, but there was a softness to her now, a quiet understanding that they were no longer just surviving. They were building something new.

Riley walked beside Ava, the two of them exchanging quiet jokes as they navigated the uneven terrain. Riley's sarcasm had become a kind of comfort, a reminder that even in the darkest moments, there was room for laughter. Ava, with her quiet strength and sharp mind, had become the glue that held them together, her knowledge of the enemy proving invaluable as they planned their next moves.

Emma and Lucy skipped ahead, their laughter echoing through the trees. The sound was a balm to Kasai's soul, a reminder that even in a world torn apart by chaos, innocence could still exist. The girls had seen more than any children should, but they carried it with a grace that left Kasai in awe.

As they walked, Kasai felt the weight of the past days settle into her bones. 72 hours. That's how long it had taken to turn their world upside down, to tear apart everything they'd known and force them into a fight for their lives. But it had also been enough time to forge unbreakable bonds, to discover strengths they didn't know they had, and to light a fire of resistance that wouldn't be extinguished.

They reached the edge of a wide field, the tall grass swaying in the breeze. In the distance, Kasai could see the faint outline of another settlement, smoke curling lazily from chimneys, and the distant murmur of voices carried on the wind.

Nora had told them about this place before they'd left the last settlement. It was a hub for survivors, a place where people from all walks of life had come together to rebuild, to resist the forces that had tried to tear them apart. It was exactly where they needed to be.

As they approached, Kasai felt a mix of anticipation and anxiety settle in her chest. She didn't know what they would find here—if the people would welcome them if they would be ready to fight. But she knew one thing for sure: they had to try.

When they reached the outskirts of the settlement, they were met by a group of guards, their weapons raised but their eyes wary rather than hostile. Kasai stepped forward, her hands raised in a gesture of peace.

"We're not here to cause trouble," she said, her voice steady. "We're survivors. And we're looking for allies."

The guards exchanged glances, and for a moment, Kasai's heart pounded in her chest. But then one of them—a tall woman with a scar running down the side of her face—lowered her weapon and nodded.

"You'd better come inside," she said. "Sounds like we've got a lot to talk about."

They were led through the settlement, the people inside watching them with a mix of curiosity and hope. The settlement was larger than the last one, with sturdy buildings and well-tended gardens. Children played in the dirt streets, their laughter a stark contrast to the hardened expressions of the adults.

Kasai felt the weight of those gazes, but she held her head high. They had faced worse than suspicion, and they had come out stronger for it.

They were brought to a large building at the center of the settlement, where a council of leaders sat around a long table. The scarred woman introduced herself as Mara, one of the leaders, and gestured for them to sit.

Kasai told their story again—the infections, the soldiers, The Nest, The Hive, and The Core. She spoke of Daniel and the experiments, of the people they'd saved and the battles they'd fought. As she spoke, the expressions of the council members shifted from skepticism to horror, and finally to grim determination.

When she finished, Mara leaned back in her chair, her eyes sharp and assessing.

"You've done more than most," Mara said quietly. "But you're right. This isn't over."

Elara nodded, her voice steady. "We need to take down the rest of the facilities. And we can't do it alone."

Mara exchanged glances with the other council members and then nodded. "You won't have to. We've been gathering resources, and training people. We've been waiting for a chance to strike back."

Kasai felt a surge of relief and hope swell in her chest. They weren't alone. The fight ahead would be hard, but they had allies now—people who believed in the same future they did.

As plans were made and alliances were forged, Kasai found herself stepping outside, the cool evening air a welcome relief against her skin. She stared up at the stars, the vast, endless sky a reminder of how small they were in the grand scheme of things. But even the smallest light could push back the darkness.

Milo joined her, his steps quiet as he leaned against the railing beside her.

"Do you think we'll win?" he asked softly, his eyes reflecting the starlight.

Kasai was silent for a moment, considering his question. The battles ahead would be brutal. They would lose people they cared about. The world might never go back to what it was.

But that didn't mean they wouldn't win.

"I think we already are," Kasai said finally, her voice soft but filled with conviction. "Because we're still here. We're still fighting. And as long as we're breathing, we've already won."

Milo smiled a small, genuine smile that warmed Kasai's heart. He reached into his pocket and pulled out a crumpled candy bar— the one he'd promised her when all of this began.

"I owe you this," he said, handing it to her.

Kasai laughed, the sound light and free. She tore open the wrapper and took a bite, savoring the sweet, simple taste. It was more than just chocolate—it was a symbol of everything they'd fought for, everything they'd survived.

They stood there in silence for a while, watching the stars, the weight of the past few days slowly lifting from their shoulders. The road ahead would be long and difficult, but they were ready.

Because they had each other.

And as long as they were together, there was nothing they couldn't face.

Kasai took a deep breath, the cool air filling her lungs, and felt a sense of peace settle over her.

They had survived 72 hours in a world that had tried to break them.

Now, it was time to live.

Epilogue

Weeks passed, and the settlements began to unite. Word of Kasai and her group spread, inspiring others to rise up, to fight back against the forces that had once seemed unstoppable. The soldiers who had terrorized the world found themselves on the defensive as more and more survivors banded together, refusing to be victims any longer.

Kasai stood at the heart of it all, her wrench now a symbol of resistance, her name a rallying cry for those who had lost everything but refused to give up.

They hadn't just survived.

They had *changed* the world.

And this was only the beginning.

ACKNOWLEDGMENTS

First and foremost, I want to thank my friend Virgil. Without him, 72 Hours wouldn't have been the same. Our countless conversations about zombies—whether we were debating survival strategies, analyzing infection spreads, or dreaming up the most absurd yet surprisingly effective ways to fight off the undead—were the spark that helped bring this story to life. It's funny how something so grim and macabre could become such a cool and meaningful thing to bond over. Whether we were theorizing about the best melee weapon, debating if we'd survive longer by heading for the woods or holing up in a fortified building, or just making up ridiculous scenarios, those moments were more than just casual conversations. They were filled with creativity, laughter, and the kind of back-and-forth that made this whole project feel real. It was during those discussions that the characters of 72 Hours started to take shape—flawed, desperate, and clinging to hope against all odds. I'm grateful not only for the inspiration Virgil provided but also for the friendship that made every discussion so much fun.

I also have to give a massive shoutout to The Walking Dead—both the game and the show. The influence it had on this book is undeniable. From the brutal realism of the characters' struggles to the raw emotional punches that made you question how much humanity you'd be willing to sacrifice just to survive—it all left a mark. The show's portrayal of loss and resilience, along with the way it explored the emotional weight of difficult choices, definitely helped shape the tone of this story. And the game, with its wrenching, player-driven decisions, stuck with me in a way that made me want to create characters in 72 Hours who would also force readers to question their own morality in a no-win situation. Watching and playing through those worlds made me realize that the apocalypse isn't just about the monsters—it's about the people. How they break, how they bond, and how sometimes, the hardest thing is keeping your humanity intact. That theme became a driving force behind this book.

To every zombie enthusiast out there—whether you've spent hours mapping out your personal survival plan, debating the practicality of a katana versus a crowbar, or simply enjoying the thrill of a good undead chase—this book is for you. There's something strangely fascinating about imagining how the world might fall apart and what it would take to make it through. Your fascination with the undead, the apocalyptic scenarios, and the desperate struggle for survival fueled my creativity and pushed me to keep asking myself: What would I do? How far would I go? Your passion for this genre made 72 Hours all the more thrilling to write.

I also want to thank every creator, writer, and storyteller who has ever dared to bring the walking dead to life. The haunting depictions of a ruined world, the morally gray characters forced into impossible choices, and the constant, suffocating tension of not knowing if you'll make it to see the next sunrise—all of it shaped my love for this genre. Whether it was through movies, games, books, or shows, your work left an impression on me, and I hope this story carries a fraction of that same haunting intensity.

Lastly, to every reader who has ever imagined themselves in the middle of a zombie apocalypse—whether you're the type to barricade yourself in a grocery store or the one who's convinced they'd take to the road with nothing but a backpack and a baseball bat—I hope you find pieces of yourself in this story. Writing 72 Hours was my own version of preparing for the end of the world—full of adrenaline, desperation, and maybe even a little hope. Thank you for stepping into this version of the apocalypse with me. I hope you enjoyed the ride.

ABOUT THE AUTHOR

La'Shayla Godfrey is a young, emerging author from Cincinnati, known for her passion for storytelling and her unique perspective. With a natural talent for capturing emotions and experiences, La'Shayla's writing reflects both her creativity and her deep connection to her roots. As a new voice in the literary world, she aims to inspire and connect with readers through powerful narratives that resonate with a wide range of audiences.

ABOUT THE PUBLISHER

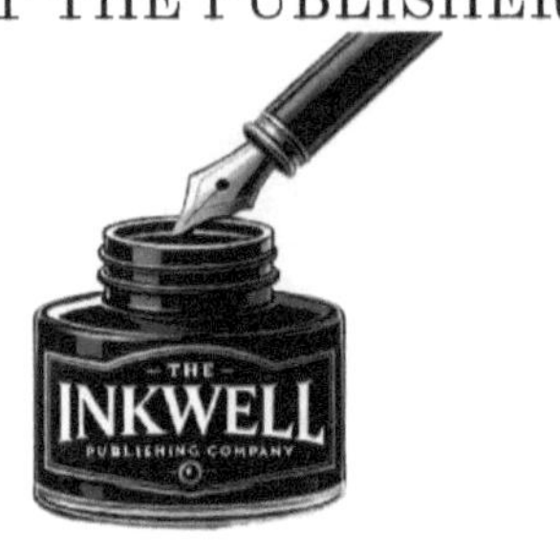

The Inkwell Publishing Company is a forward-thinking literary hub dedicated to reshaping the publishing landscape. The company is driven by the belief that ideas have the power to inspire change, spark creativity, and connect humanity. At The Inkwell, authors are empowered to share their unique voices, and readers are invited into a community that values thought-provoking stories and meaningful engagement.

More than just a publisher, The Inkwell Publishing Company is a platform for innovation and collaboration. It champions new ways of thinking about literature and publishing, challenging traditional norms to create an inclusive, transformative space for creators and audiences alike. Through its commitment to quality, originality, and authenticity, The Inkwell is shaping the future of storytelling—one idea at a time.